HER VILLAINS
A FANTASY REVERSE HAREM NOVEL

JADE PRESLEY

CONTENT WARNING

This book contains some depictions of emotional abuse, violence and gore, and sexual content with multiple consenting partners. I've taken every effort to handle these issues sensitively, but if any of these elements could be considered triggering to you, please take note.

Copyright © 2022 by Jade Presley. All rights reserved. This book or any portion thereof may not be reproduced or used in any manner whatsoever without the express written permission of the publisher except for the use of brief quotations in a book review. This is a work of fiction. Names, characters, businesses, places, events and incidents are either the products of the author's imagination or used in a fictitious manner. Any resemblance to actual persons, living or dead, or actual events is purely coincidental. This book is licensed for your personal enjoyment only. This book may not be resold or given away to other people. If you would like to share this book with another person, please purchase an additional copy for each person you'd like to share it with. Thank you for respecting the author's work.

For all the Marvel fans who need a little extra spice

PROLOGUE
CARI

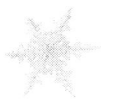

My wedding day is cursed.

I've lived my entire life under the stars, but the sun shines brightly as I walk toward my three soon-to-be husbands.

Of course, I've known for years that my bonding ceremony would be like walking to my death.

What else can it be, when I'm marrying the enemy?

I step in front of the high priestess, my three betrothed standing with military stiffness before her. Their faces are hidden by their All Plane helmets—maroon and gold with a sun emblem blazoned across the forehead. But each one is incredibly tall and well-built beneath their tight-fitting royal armor.

"You understand what I'm asking of you, daughter?" my father's voice echoes in the back of my mind, the memory of our conversation last night replacing the wedding scene before me.

Asking? He isn't asking. The king of the Shattered Isle asks for nothing.

He's demanding. Ordering.

And as his sole heir? I'm expected to obey.

Some missions, like the time he'd send me to the Onyx City at the edge of our island to eradicate a mite infestation, were pure fun and adventure.. I'd dispersed of the dozen parasitic creatures before they could nest or threaten too many lives. Other times, like when he sent me to Sand's Swallow—an impoverished village on our island—to help jump-start its harvest, were heart-wrenching.

But this mission?

Can I do this?

I tip my chin up. "I will marry the princes of the All Plane."

"Your marriage will bring peace to the two realms." *He shifts his massive form on his throne. The obsidian chair is smooth and polished with intricately carved constellations decorated into the rock. It has served as the Shattered Isle king's throne for ages, with each ruler adding their own set of stars to it when they ascend the throne.* "Our two kingdoms will no longer know the centuries-long war that has cost both realms buckets of blood."

I nod.

"You will serve the princes in any way they desire." *His eyebrows raise as he looks down at me.*

"Yes, Father," *I say from where I kneel on the stone floor before the dais on which he sits.*

"Whatever they want," *he continues.* "We have been enemies for longer than this world can remember. Their ancestors are the reason our Isle is shattered. The Great War broke our land, sepa-

rated us from them, sweeping in that black ocean to keep us contained. Their thirst for blood is the reason I keep our people under such control, to protect them." Anger colors his tone, and his massive fist tightens on his golden scepter.

I bite my tongue, knowing exactly what kind of punishment I'll receive if I speak up for our people again. Speak out against Father's restrictive curfews, the taxes he collects to fund his armies that leave the people starving, the fear of young males being ripped from their families to join an army before they're big enough to hold a sword.

My people deserve better. And if completing this mission will loosen Father's grip on them, then I will do it.

"The orders they deliver may differ vastly from that of our traditions," he continues.

I swallow hard, the only show of nerves I'll allow. The All Plane bred warriors of the most lethal kind—brutish and brash. Our Shattered Isle warriors are known for cunning and stealth, but are no less deadly than the All Plane warriors who deign themselves saviors of the realms. They rule with endless armies and wipe out anyone they deem too different from their own kind.

Like us. Shattered Islers who draw strength from the stars and the moon and the raging black sea.

The All Plane draws their power from the sun and warmth and solid earth.

We couldn't be more different.

What will the All Plane princes ask me to do? As their wife, I'll be expected to accommodate any and all desires, but I'd be lying if I said I'm not a little concerned with what they might demand of me.

"I'll make them happy." For my people. I'll do anything to help them, save them.

"You'll have to do more than that," he says.

"I'll make them love me." I recite the plan we've gone over for weeks. Months. Years.

"Their love for you must grow wider and deeper than our beloved sea." He rises from his throne, stepping down the stone stairs to meet me. I rise at his motion, tipping my head up to look at him. "For our people, for the fate of the worlds," he says, two fingers under my chin. "You must make them believe you are everything they have ever searched for."

"Yes, Father."

"Love is like a blade winking in the moonlight—it blinds before it kills."

I nod.

He'd raised an assassin princess. Strong, cunning, deadly. All wrapped in a pretty package no one would ever suspect.

"I won't ask you if you can *do this," he continues, dropping his hand from my chin. "I know you can. Because I know you understand the alternative if you fail." He glances to his most trusted second in command—General Payne—who delights in torture and blood. The garish creature grins at me, teeth like sharpened claws, and a shiver skates down my spine.*

If I fail, General Payne will make my death last for nights.

And if the princes suspect me for even a second, they'll *kill me. I'm the enemy, after all. I always have been. My people always have been.*

Failure isn't an option.

"I understand what I have to do," I say, willing strength into my voice.

Marry the princes of the All Plane.

Journey to their realm.

Kill each of them before we reach the palace.

And somehow not get caught.

The fate of our people hangs in the balance.

What can possibly go wrong?

"With the braiding of power, touch, and spoken vow," the high priestess says, snapping me back to the present. "I implore you all to make the bond official."

"Bonded for life," we each say in unison. "I will protect and cherish my mate until the breath leaves my lungs." We finish the words required of us, and the priestess offers us each a dip of her head.

"You are bonded," she says, and turns to the crowd of my people. Some offer well-wishing looks, but none cheer or clap or jump up and down. And I can't blame them. This is a radical move they never saw coming. Yet, there is hope in my people's eyes. Hope for a new era to follow this unprecedented union.

One of peace.

I *wish* peace could be so easily gained with a wedding, a few bonds, and a future chained to my new husbands.

Too bad the price for peace can only be bought with blood.

1
CARI

The All Plane princes' sky ship is unlike any I've boarded before. It's a glistening silver palace built for luxury and adventure. Nothing like the few common vessels we have for sky travel. Their sky ship has rooms and hallways that go on for miles. Each one is more lavish than the next. So, the rumors about the All Plane's wealth are true—it's unending, if this is just *one* of many sky ships they own.

I barely feel the machine rumble as it catapults us into the sky, and my heart leaps into my throat as I watch our assent from the floor-to-ceiling windows. My beautiful, obsidian ocean shrinks the higher we climb, until it is nothing but a thin, sparkling line of black beneath us.

Something pricks my chest, a sharp twinge of regret as my home disappears. My father offered me no warm goodbyes, not that I expected him to. Gessi, my one friend and handmaiden, shared tears with me the night before when we said our goodbyes. I will miss her most of all, and the pit in my stomach is telling me I'll never see her or my beloved ocean again.

As the vessel takes us higher, a cerulean blue sky filled with white fluffy clouds replaces the view of my Shattered Isle. I've never ventured past our island's borders, and now I'm being flown away toward the opposite side of the sea where the other elemental realms rest.

I turn away from the massive windows, my flowing gown of red silk dusting the sleek floors. My husbands are still in their armor, two of them not even bothering to glance back as they hurry down an adjoining hallway.

The other lingers at my right side. I can only make out a pair of full lips since he still wears his helmet, and he parts them—

"The dining hall is prepped," a male voice says, drawing my attention. A thin, younger male wearing the All Plane crest on simple clothes stands at attention. This must be one of many staff onboard the sky ship. "Shall I escort you?"

"That won't be necessary," my new husband answers, his voice strong but calm and respectful as he addresses his staff. "Thank you, though, Cansil."

The younger male bows, then disappears down the hallway.

"Come," he says, extending his arm for me.

I swallow hard, but take his arm, the muscles rippling beneath my touch as he leads me down the hallway. Apprehension climbs up my spine as I follow him. Sure, the staff member said the dining hall was ready, but who's to say they haven't prepped it for my torture? My father had told me countless stories about how much the princes excel at torturing their enemies. What if that's what they have in mind for our honeymoon—

"Steel," he says, his voice lowered almost to a whisper between us. He removes his helmet with his free hand, gripping it by his side as he looks down at me.

My heart stutters as his sapphire blue eyes lock with mine. His hair is golden, like the sun he worships, and is carefully styled in a short, elegant cut. He's cleanshaven, showing off a strong jaw, and those full lips curve into a genuine smile. He arches a brow. "Steel," he says again.

I furrow my brow, wondering if he's warning me not to steal anything aboard this ship. Does he truly think so little of Shattered Islers that he'd think I would start pocketing the cutlery at dinner?

His smile deepens as we walk, and I hate that butterflies flap in my stomach at the sight.

"This is the part where you tell me *your* name," he says, turning another corner.

I huff a laugh, unable to contain it. "Your name is Steel?" I ask. It wasn't like the high priestess had listed our proper names at the ceremony. Such things were considered unnecessary in the eyes of the bonding. Steel nods. "Cari," I say.

"*Cah-ree*," he draws out my name, testing it on his tongue, and warm shivers burst over my skin. "Beautiful name."

He turns into a large room with golden lights hanging from the ceiling, casting a dozen rich wooden tables in a warm glow. One male sits at the head of the centermost table, hair as black as night with a goatee to match, his eyes nearly as dark and menacing as he refuses to look up at our entry. Another male is sitting on the other side of the table, his hair golden like Steel's but sheered against the sides of his head and longer on the top, and he has two lightning bolt tattoos inked down the right side of his neck.

"I did ask your father to permit a pre-bonding-ceremony meeting, so we could at least learn each other's names, but he refused," Steel says as he leads us to the table. It's topped with roasted meats and veggies, greens and soups, and enough bread and cheese to feed half my island.

"Would it have made a difference?" I ask as he pulls out a chair for me, settling me into it. My heart is racing as I eye the other two brothers—my new husbands. The dark-haired one is looking at me with the disgust I expected from all of them while the other has nothing but pure curiosity and challenge in his eyes.

"It would've been nice to at least know each other's names before we were bonded for life," Steel says, choosing the chair to my right. "Wouldn't it?"

I shrug, but can't help the relieved sigh that leaves my lips as he starts filling my plate with food. At least, for now, it doesn't seem like torture is on the menu, but I don't dare let my guard drop.

"What were you afraid of, little wife?" the one with the lightning bolts along his neck asks me before tearing off a hunk of meat from some animal leg. He smirks, his light blue eyes trailing the lines of my face.

"I wasn't—"

He points that animal leg at me. "Don't deny it," he says. "I saw you practically shudder with relief at the sight of this table. Now, you were either afraid and relieved with what you found, or you haven't been fed properly in days." He licks his lips, eyes churning with fire. "Seeing your

HER VILLAINS

delectable curves under all that silk, I'm betting on the first."

Heat floods my cheeks and I press my lips together. I could leap over this table right now, draw on my power, and end him before he could finish his meal. But the other two would have my head before I got the chance to finish them too.

Patience.

First, I have to earn their trust.

Then, when their guard is down, I'll strike at them one at a time.

"Tor," Steel chides as he piles food onto his fork. "It's her first night with us, can you take it easy—"

"I am taking it easy," Tor says, cocking a brow at his brother. He leans back in his seat, the leathers he wears under his arm stretching tight over tons of muscle. They must've changed right before coming here. Steel still dons his wedding clothes, having skipped his chance to change in order to guide me here. "I'm trying to get to know her."

Steel sighs, continuing with his food.

I take small bites, trying not to look to the head of the table. I can practically feel the weight of the hateful stare from the dark-haired one. It matches the hate I feel in my heart, but I'm much better at hiding it.

Tor leans his elbows on the table, drawing himself closer to the middle, eyes on me. "Tell me," he says, his voice rough, low. "Did you think we were going to stretch you out along this table and use you for our own personal feast?"

My lips part at his words, tendrils of heat shooting up my spine.

Tor smirks as he eyes my neck. "Is that what had your pulse racing when you sat down?"

Words tangle in my throat. *No one* speaks to me like that. Ever.

And my body *reacts* to the image he paints.

The idea of all three of their hands on me at once...I can barely imagine it.

As princess of the Shattered Isle, any suitable partner had always been too afraid of my father's wrath to ask for my hand in courtship, and those who *were* brave enough to steal a few intimate moments with me under the blanket of darkness were always too afraid they'd break me.

The only true pleasure I've experienced has been by my own hand, but looking at my new husbands? I have no doubts the things they could do to me. Especially if they saw me as anything other than the delicate, defenseless princess the world viewed me as—the mask my father ensured our people and those across the sea saw.

Not the weapon I truly am.

"Tor," Steel chides again, and I blink out of my mental spiraling. Steel turns to me, his features apologetic, which almost surprises me more than what Tor had said. "Forgive him, wife, he's—"

"Don't," the dark-haired one says, his harsh tone jolting my senses. "Don't call her that."

"*Talon*," Steel warns, and my eyes dart from him to Talon and back again. I dip my head slightly, just enough to cast the role of the wounded, docile princess. "She is our *wife* and as such is now an All Plane princess.

Tor pauses his eating, cocking a brow at Steel's tone toward Talon. Not a silent order to stop, but an intrigued look that has high hopes for a good brawl.

Talon grips his knife and fork so hard, I'm surprised he hasn't launched across that table and jabbed one in my eye already.

He could try, but he'd be sorely disappointed when I removed his hand for him.

"She is a princess of the Shattered Isle," Talon spits. "Raised by our enemy, which makes her *our* enemy."

I flinch, the move not totally for show. Talon's tone is harsh, rough, and raw, like the hurts of the past between our peoples have cut him deeply. In this, we're the same. He's just on the wrong side of it.

"Careful," Steel warns, and my lungs tighten at the new tone from the previously gentle voice. "Father decreed this union. A high priestess blessed and bonded us by our powers. You don't have to like it, brother, but Cari is now *ours*."

Lava soars through my veins at the verbal claiming, and I try my best to shove the sensation away. With the way he's defending me, Steel's trust may be the easiest to earn out of the three.

"She does look rather fun," Tor says, leaning back in his chair and cleaning his nails with a dagger, his plate clear and wine goblet half-empty.

I admire the weapon from where I sit, noting the rubies laid into the hilt that flicker in the light. I wonder if each ruby represents a kill for him, and then just as quickly wonder if those kills were my people or those from other warring lands.

"Not at all what I pictured when Father said we had to marry a Shattered Isler." Tor continues, almost as if he's trying to change the subject between Steel and Talon.

I tilt my head, wondering what he'd been expecting? I certainly hadn't dreamed the All Plane princes would look like descendants of sun gods—all golden skin over tons of corded muscle, each of them radiating unmatched power—but I suppose I *should've*. They are prized warriors, after all, and indeed look the part.

Talon rubs his hands over his face, shaking his head. "I will not stand by and watch her tear us apart from the inside out." His tone is low, almost a growl. A wave of exhaustion rolls over me at the idea of winning his trust. It will be nearly impossible. He glares at me, a twisted grin on his lips. "And the high priestess bonded you to *each* of the All Plane princes," he says. "You do know what that means, don't you?"

Ice skates down my spine. The fourth brother.

The mere thought of *that* prince kept me up tossing and turning for days this past week. The fourth prince, exiled from his homeland because of one nefarious action or another. Rumors say he's been on the run from the All Plane's warriors for over a year. If they catch him? He'll be my husband too, by law—already is, technically.

The All Plane warriors are renowned for their abilities to imprison traitors and dispense justice, but he's thwarted their every attempt at capture. If he ever surfaces, he would prove an *actual* threat to my mission.

Talon's dark eyes damn near twinkle as he watches me put the pieces together. "Maybe we'll finally find Lock and give you to him. You wouldn't survive the night—"

HER VILLAINS

"Brother," Tor says, sliding his dagger into a sheath at his side. "Steel is right. She is our wife. Our mate. It is now our duty to protect and accept—"

"No," Talon cuts him off, shoving away from the table. "The priestess might've said the words, but we all know the bond isn't recognized by our powers *or* those above until we consummate the union." He curls his lips at me. "And I have *zero* interest in that." He spins on his heels, hurrying out of the room as if I'd set fire to the table.

The blow hits dead center in my chest, anger gathering there to soothe the hurt. He acts as if *I'm* this hideous creature with razor-sharp teeth and bloody-tipped claws, not some princess in a flowing dress that doesn't even show off my breasts.

"Forgive him," Steel says, his tone switching back to that soft-as-silk tenor. I turn to look at him. His firm jaw is taut, showing his frustration, but the rest of his body is relaxed as he sits close to me. "This is new to him. To all of us. I'm sure you have reservations about us as well."

My eyebrows raise at that, shock flowing through me. I didn't think any of the All Plane warriors would spare half a second thinking about what *I* thought of any of this.

Steel offers me a genuine smile, one that lights up his eyes. Night damn my body, I can't help but react to the kind warrior. He's clearly the heart of these princes, showing more compassion in the last five minutes than other two showed in the last few hours.

"And don't let Talon's threats of using Lock against you frighten you," Steel continues. "We haven't seen our brother in…" He rolls up his eyes, as if he's calculating the number in his mind.

"A year," Tor offers, a hint of sadness and longing in his voice.

I wonder how their brother has managed to escape them for an entire year, but Steel draws my attention again.

"Yes, a year," Steel says. "Lock is the least of our worries right now." He motions to my barely touched plate. "You should eat, wife," he says.

I do as he says, mostly because I have no idea what to say to either of them. This isn't at all what I expected. I expected torture or isolation from my enemies, not feasts and kind words and teasing. Even Talon, with his threats and open hostility, left me to dine with his brothers instead of throwing me in some cage to be dealt with later.

And when I realize what will likely come *after* dining, I slow down even more. I savor each bite, my nerves coiling inside me. Tonight, they'll expect me to consummate the bond with one of them, or each of them. I'm not exactly sure.

The visual of all three of them claiming me at the same time fills my mind again—a purely hedonistic scene with an endless supply of muscles and mouths, tongues and teeth. Warm tendrils tremble in my core, followed by a heavy dose of shame. How can I possibly imagine such things? I force the fantasy away, and do my best to remember what I'm here for.

Tor pushes away from the table, and a smirk shapes his lips as he stops to look down at me. I have to tip my head back to meet his gaze, he's that damn tall. They *all* are. His light blue eyes rake down my body with a searing gaze, lust flickering over them as if he can see through the eons of fabric covering my body. I feel his look like a brand, hot and heady, but somehow manage to not look away.

"As much as I'd love to keep watching you eat, little wife," he says, his voice like liquid velvet, "I have matters to attend to on the sixth floor."

"Of course," Steel says, tensing briefly. He quickly shakes it off, smiling down at me. "We're fine without you, Tor. We don't need a chaperone."

Tor doesn't move at Steel's obvious dismissal. He seems content to stand there and stare at me.

"What are you looking at, husband?" I say, letting the new title roll off my tongue in the same seductive tone he'd given me seconds before.

That mischievous smile returns. "The before picture," he says. I swallow hard as he cuts a playful gaze to Steel. "Don't break her too quickly, brother," he says, and winks at me.

2
STEEL

"You are not at all what I expected," I admit with a laugh as I sit next to Cari at the dining table.

I'm grateful Tor left, leaving me to be alone with our new wife. Talon had already expressed his disgust, and while Tor means well, his playful barbing likely would take Cari some time to get used to.

She blinks a few times, quickly setting down her third leg of meat, and wipes at her lips with a napkin. "What were you expecting?" Her voice is much softer than her eyes, which are two beautifully dark orbs as hard as the moonstone rocks that shape her isle.

My eyes fall to that napkin at her lips and to the tongue she sweeps across them. Fuck, she's gorgeous. The endless silk of her dress can't hide her mouthwatering curves or her glittering blue skin, and her full lips are nothing short of tempting. But it's her eyes I can't get enough of because they're hiding something. I'm not sure what, but I'm dying to find out.

HER VILLAINS

"We've heard of the Shattered Isle, but only one of us has ever been there before, and that was before the war. We have tomes on the Great War that separated our realms, and the illustrations…" I stop myself short, not wanting to offend her. Regardless of Talon's reservations, when I take an oath, I stand by it. If our union brings peace to the restless realms, then I'm for it. And I'll do everything in my power to make sure she's protected and happy while we do it.

She smiles then, and the breath stalls in my lungs. This smile differs from the ones she's offered so far. It's not timid or shy. This one is full and real and just this side of trouble.

"Let me guess," she says, pushing away her plate. She's eaten over three helpings from the kitchen, and by the *sun,* I loved watching her take every bite. "The illustrations in those tomes colored us with horns and fangs and claws?"

I choke out a laugh, reaching for the crystal wine in my goblet. I take a fast drink, setting down the cup. "Yes," I admit.

Surprise lights her eyes.

I lean closer to her, catching her scent, a mixture of the sea and stars and night-blooming flowers. My cock twitches, a primal urge rising inside me to find out if she tastes as good as she smells.

"I know you don't have any reason to trust me yet, Cari," I say, shifting in my chair and mentally telling my dick to calm down. She isn't ready yet, and I hold no pleasure in taking a female who has no interest in being claimed. "But I will never lie to you."

She visibly swallows, studying me. After a few moments, she blinks away the look, leaning close to me too, so close our noses nearly touch. She peels back her lips, and for a second I think she's going to put me out of my misery and kiss me. Instead, she bares her teeth.

"No fangs," she says, falling back in her chair.

The breath rushes out of my lungs, and my dick groans in protest. I haven't wanted someone this badly in ages. Sure, I've fucked plenty of willing females, but they were always vying for my crown, not my heart, and each one I took to bed knew they could have neither.

Maybe it has something to do with the bonding, something to do with our powers testing and braiding with each other during the ceremony, but I *want* Cari on a level that has me aching to heft her onto this table and sink inside her right here and now.

I spare half a thought to wonder how Tor's and Talon's powers reacted to hers at the ceremony. My infinite strength had felt like a shield to her flicker of ice, and I couldn't wait to see what all she could actually do with her power. Surely Talon—with his genius ability to create—felt the goodness in her? He was just being stubborn. And it was clear that Tor was itching to test his lightning against her. But for now, it was just us, and I preferred it that way.

"I still would've taken care of you," I finally say, hoping she can't hear the need in my voice. I've lived some two-hundred years and I'm acting like a youngling drooling over a pretty female in a dress.

She arches a brow at me. "Is that so?"

"It wouldn't have mattered to me if you had claws or fangs," I say. "Or if you were the monster from the storybooks. I'm a man of my word, and I promised to protect you, cherish you." I inhale a deep breath, letting my eyes wander over her body for the briefest of moments before returning to her eyes. "And I intend to do that."

The slightest shudder shakes her body, and I can't stop my grin. So she *is* affected by me too. Good to know, since my new wife seems like the sea she loves so much—full of secrets and as changing as the tides.

"You're not what I expected either," she admits, dipping her head to the staff member who clears her tray of food and refills our goblets with sparkling wine.

I cringe. "I can't imagine," I say. "If our stories are wrong about your people, there is no telling what yours says about us."

Her eyes go distant for a few moments, and I imagine her in her youth, in her palace's library, a tutor pacing before her while drilling lessons into her brain. "You're depicted as warriors," she says, returning her attention to me. "But none with the kindness you've already shown me." Her shoulders dip a fraction, and I can't tell if she's upset that I've been kind to her or sad that the stories from our peoples were wrong. "Tor was right," she admits. "When you brought me in here, I thought it was to torture me."

"I'm sorry you thought that," I say, daring to take her hand in mine, her glorious blue skin contrasting beautifully against my gold. "Lies and fabrications go hand in hand with war." I'm relieved when she doesn't flinch at my touch or pull away. I rub my thumb over her palm. "We're here today to correct that. To shed truth on the lies fed to both our peoples over the last few centuries."

Intrigue lights up her features, and I slip my thumb beneath the long sleeve of her dress, teasing the delicate skin of her wrist. Her intake of breath is fuel for my already aching cock, and I shift again, taking a deep breath to find patience.

Cari may be ours, but I will not take her until she asks me to.

"I hope you're right," she says.

"Do you doubt me?" I ask, still playing with her wrist. It's her turn to shift in her chair, and I grin.

"I do not," she says a little too quickly. "But centuries-old wounds can be hard to mend, regardless of marriages."

I nod. She's not wrong.

"We have to start somewhere," I say, almost as if I'm speaking to my father again. Pleading with him to end the pain and suffering between our two great realms. It wasn't an easy feat to convince him to agree to this marriage, and even when we bring Cari home in three weeks' time, I'm not sure if he'll accept it. I'm nothing if not determined to prove him wrong. "Or the healing can never begin," I finish.

"And you want it to heal?" she asks. "The suffering between your realm and mine?"

"Of course," I say. "The universe is too great a place to waste it in conflict over cultural differences."

Her eyebrows raise, just a tiny bit of shock shaping her features.

"Tell me," I continue. "Tell me about the Shattered Isle."

"What do you want to know?" she asks.

"Everything. Anything," I say. "Tell me the stories only a true Shattered Isler would know."

HER VILLAINS

A small, effortless grin shapes her lips, and hope fills my heart. I hate that she thought we'd treat her as a prisoner, as an enemy. I want to erase that fear from her mind as quickly as possible—but of course, Talon's hatred definitely isn't helping my efforts.

"My handmaiden," she starts, then shakes her head, her long black hair shifting on her shoulders. "My *friend* Gessi and me loved watching the midnight sea from a secluded cove on the farthest edge of the beach."

Her dark eyes twinkle with the memory as I hang on her every word.

"Father's guards always thought we were in my room, but I knew how to sneak out of the palace. She'd pack a satchel full of lemon cakes and chocolate biscuits, and we'd sit under the protection of that cove, hidden from our responsibilities. We weren't a princess and a handmaiden there, we were just two friends, listening to the crashing waves and counting falling stars." A sadness flickers over her eyes, but she blinks it away.

"Do many Shattered Islers take part in the pleasures of the beach?" I ask.

"No," she answers quickly. "Father has a curfew for our people ensuring they return to their homes well before the sun rises, for their protection," she says. "What Gessi and I did was reckless. We were caught once…" Her voice trails off, a shudder shaking her body.

"What happened?" I ask, my free hand curling into a fist. Our own father's punishments weren't easy by any means, but my brothers and I were quick learners—

"Father's general," she says, shrugging. "He's a brutal creature who delights in putting wounds where no one can openly see them. He ensured we wouldn't break the rules again. After all, I'm my people's princess. They need an example to follow. If they don't follow the rules…" She unlinks our hands, rubbing hers over her arms as if she's soothing an old wound. "Anyway," she continues. "The only thing the general's punishment did was ensure we were never caught again." A mischievous smile shakes away the darkness lining her eyes. "And we never were."

I scan her features, her body, as if I can find the old scars from whatever this general did to her and erase them. She speaks about it so casually, and with her mention of torture earlier, it's almost as if she's used to that kind of treatment. Anger snakes hot through my blood, a call for retribution ringing in my heart. She's ours. Mine. She will not be punished again for something as simple as sneaking out to enjoy the ocean.

"Do you have beaches in the All Plane?" she asks.

I take a breath, letting the need for revenge leak from my body. She's here now, and no one will ever touch her like that again. "Not anything as grand as your midnight sea," I say. "But there are rivers that sparkle like the stars you love so much when the sun hits them right."

She leans forward, smiling at the picture I've painted.

We continue swap stories for hours, and it isn't until she yawns that I realize how long we've sat here. "You must be exhausted," I say, and internally scold myself.

She's used to staying awake all night and sleeping during the day, and while I knew she'd have to change her schedule to live with us, I hadn't planned on keeping her up the entire day. The sun is now setting, painting the sky outside the windows a burnt orange color.

But she's just so damn easy to talk to. She listens, not in the way one does out of obligation or duty, but out of genuine interest. She asked questions and seemed fascinated at comparing the differences in our histories, and there had been many. So many lies told from both sides.

"I am," she admits, yawning again. "I'm sorry, husband," she says. "I don't want to stop the fun we're having."

I smile at that, pushing back from the table and offering her my hand. She doesn't even know half the fun we can have when we retire to the bedroom we've fashioned for her. But, of course, that's only if she wants me.

"Come, wife," I say. I'm getting used to the term that Talon scolded me for using before. "Let me show you to your room."

She takes my hand, following me out of the quiet dining hall.

"Not *your* room?" Cari asks a little timidly. The question sets my blood on fire.

"Would you rather sleep in my room?" I ask. She furrows her brow, clearly caught in a battle between what she wants to say and what she thinks she *should* say. I stop in the middle of the hallway, tipping her chin up so she meets my eyes. "There is no wrong answer, Cari," I say and realize I love saying her name just as much as her title. "This is new to you. To all of us. I will not force you to consummate our bond tonight. It's always your choice with me."

But with my brothers? I hate to admit that I'm not sure how hard they'll push to complete the bonding process, but at least for tonight, she's in my care.

Her throat bobs a little, and her bottom lip trembles. I smooth the pad of my thumb over that lip, and a stuttered sigh slips past. Fuck, I want to taste those lips.

"My room, please," she says. "For tonight," she adds as I starting walking again, leading us down to the second level of the ship.

"Of course," I say, hating the disappointment in my veins.

I want her to want me just as badly, I remind myself as I push open the door to her room. The disappointment all but disappears as her mouth drops open at the sight before her.

"This... this is my room?" she asks, stepping inside, her feet meeting lush red carpets as her eyes take in the elegantly decorated space.

A bed fit for a queen is tucked against the farthest wall, piled high with every manner of silk and cashmere and comfort we can afford. A black walnut end table sits on either side, a stack of books decorating the top. I walk over to the closet on the opposite side of the room, waving a hand in front of the sensor there. The doors fly open, and her second gasp is as delicious as the first.

"This is all yours as well," I say, showing her the closet full of clothes and shoes and jewels. "If anything isn't to your liking, all you have to do is tell me."

"It's beautiful," she says almost to herself as she runs her fingers over a pair of tight leathers with the All Plane crest over the stomach. "It's too much, Steel."

I nearly groan at the sound of my name rolling off her tongue and I suddenly realize I prefer that much more than *husband*. There was a vulnerability in the way she said it, almost as if she didn't mean to let it slip past her lips.

I meet her in the closet, once again smoothing my fingers along hers. "You are my princess now," I say. "Nothing is too much."

A flush dusts her cheeks, and I pull away from her. If I stay in here much longer, I'll bend her over the cushioned bench separating the closet and make her *scream* my name. I head back into the main room as quickly as I can, cursing the bond between us for making my mind so one-tracked.

I point to another door across the room. "Bathing chamber," I grind out the words, unable to stop the flood of images spilling into my mind. Her stripping out of that dress and bathing in the stone shower, her breasts dripping wet, nipples peaked for sucking—

Stop. I close my eyes for a moment, willing myself to find calm.

"Thank you," she says, and there is such a genuine surprise in her tone that I open my eyes.

"Of course," I say again. We linger in a tensed silence for a few moments and I'm about to bid her goodnight—

"Do you want to stay with me?" she asks softly.

"Yes," I say on a breath. "But you don't have to—"

"I admit I'm not ready to consummate our bond," she cuts me off. "But I'm not ready to say goodnight to you either."

What does that mean?

Does it matter?

No.

"If you want me to tell you stories all night, I will. Or, if you want me to hold you and nothing more, I will. You need only ask."

A smile lights up her face, an almost giddy excitement that has my nerves tangling. And how the hell is that possible? I'm a grown male, an All Plane prince and warrior who has spent many a night in a female's bed. Why is this one so different?

"Good," she says and turns back toward the closet. "May I change?"

"I am not your master," I say. "You don't have to ask my permission." What had her life been like on the Shattered Isle to feel the need to ask me such a question? Or was it simply because she still feared me and my brothers to be the monsters she'd grown up hearing about?

"Are you going to change?" she asks, and I blink down at the armor still decorating my body.

"I'll be back in a few minutes," I say and hurry out of the room.

The sun gods smile on me, because I don't run into either of my brothers on my way to and from my room. I change in record time, everything in my blood willing me to get back to Cari, consummation or not. I just want to be with her, and that should probably worry me more than it does, but I just can't seem to care.

She's mine.

She's ours.

And I want nothing more than to make her feel like she belongs.

When I return, I shut her door behind me, quietly locking it. Not that my brothers will decide to join us—even though that is their full right to do—but she's already expressed she's not ready. And while I know my brothers are honorable men, Tor definitely doesn't have the patience I do, and Talon? Fuck, he'll chew her up just to spit her out.

At least, with me, she's safe.

And the relief in my chest at the sight of her in her cobalt silk pajamas? Her hair fully down and cascading over her shoulders as she sits on the bed? I know she'll *always* be safe with me.

"Where would you like me?" I ask as her gaze lingers on my black cotton pants and sleeveless shirt. I point to the array of comfortable chairs and chaise lounge across the room, but she shakes her head.

"Here?" She smooths her hand over the spot next to her, and I have to count to ten before I walk toward the bed.

I sink onto the mattress, and in a move too natural to be forced, I extend my arm. She instantly tucks herself against me, and I sigh at the contact, at the slight weight of her against my body.

"Are you disappointed in me, husband?" she asks, her voice heavy with sleep.

I shift enough to look down at her. "Not at all," I say. "Why would I be?"

She yawns again, and I laugh. "Because I'm not ready—"

"Hey," I cut her off. "I will never force you. Is the bond screaming at me for completion? Yes." She trembles at my words. "But I will never take what isn't willingly given. You are my mate. I want your trust, your heart, *and* your body."

She relaxes against me, running her hands over my abdomen, then my chest, making lazy loops. I trace the beautiful ink on her left arm—the night-blooming flowers beacons of temptation begging me to trace the petals with my tongue. I breathe deeply as we lay there, innocently touching and relaxing into the silence between us.

"Good," she says again, her head lying heavier on my chest than moments before, her body giving in to exhaustion. "Because…" The pauses between her words lengthen, and I have to bite back laughter at how stubborn she is to stay awake when she clearly needs sleep. "I want to at least be fully awake…when you take me."

Her words send heat straight to my cock, and if her hand on my thigh was two inches to the right, she would feel how badly I want to sink into her right this second.

But her soft, even breathing calms those thoughts.

I hold her while she sleeps, relishing this first step.

She awoke this morning as the daughter of my enemy, but she sleeps now as my wife, a princess of the All Plane.

And we have the rest of our lives to discover each other.

3
CARI

I startle awake, wondering why I can't hear the ocean outside my window. My heart races as my mind catches up and my eyes fall on the sleeping male beside me.

Steel.

He's on his back, a muscled arm under his head, the other wrapped around my shoulders, holding me tight against his side. He's so warm, his scent of fresh soap and pine curling around me in an intoxicating way.

He stayed with me all day and night yesterday. We talked, comparing histories and customs. We even *laughed* together. Definitely not the first night I'd imagined after marrying my enemies.

I shift slightly against him, unable to deny the way his body makes mine feel—hot and achy. I can't deny the attraction. I'd be a liar if I said *any* of my husbands weren't beyond gorgeous. But, I didn't expect it. Didn't expect to *want* Steel as badly as I do. Hell, even Tor, with his brazen looks and warrior charm, or Talon with his anger and hate.

I want all of them, if only to know what it's like. And that alone is enough to have shame coating my skin like layer of grime. They are my enemies. They are responsible for countless Shattered Isle deaths.

But Steel? Damn him. He'd burrowed under my skin last night. Especially with his hope for his people *and* mine. The way he accepted my people as his, and vice versa. How the hell am I going to kill someone so... good?

He can't be good. His people have murdered mine for centuries.

The voice in my mind sounds more like my father's than my own.

But, according to Steel, only one of them has ever been to my realm before and it was before the war started.

Something isn't adding up, because my father had told me hundreds of stories of them leading their armies into surrounding villages and mowing over them like wheat in a field. How can I believe Steel over my father after only one night?

Because he's a good male.

The answer presents itself so damn clearly, and from the test I offered last night, he *is* a good male. I'd been more than ready to climb the prince like the tree he is, if not a little tiredly, but instead, I asked him to wait.

I absolutely did not expect him to *allow* my request.

To respect me not being ready.

But he did.

Wholeheartedly.

He'd held me, felt nothing but silk between us, and still refrained from trying to solidify our new bond.

How can the nightmare my father painted the princes to be fit into this male beside me? The gentle warrior who has shown me nothing but kindness, acceptance, and patience? Who painted such a beautiful picture of peace and prosperity between our realms for the future?

Maybe he's an anomaly.

Maybe the horror stories of our warring people come from those like Talon or Tor or their estranged brother Lock... wherever he may be.

It's been one night. You don't have a clue who this male really is.

Guilt creeps up and settles in my chest, a war of emotions battling inside me. The ones screaming at me to jump out of this bed right this second and cut off whatever affections I might be developing for Steel, and the ones cooing at me to settle in, to explore and delight and devour him.

Night damn me, I stay right where I am.

I relish the relaxed warmth I've never experienced before. The few males I'd been with in my isle never stuck around long enough to hug me, let alone hold me. Those rare occurrences when I took a break from the restrictive life of assassin training to escape for a few moments with whoever was bold enough to try with me. Too many of the quick encounters occurred in back alleys where my father's guards couldn't find me, but even if we'd been in a bed, they still would've raced off after finishing, fearful of my father's axe.

But not Steel.

He sleeps soundly with me in his arms as if I'm someone he can trust, someone he doesn't have to fear because of my father's position.

I settle deeply against his strong, broad chest, and tell myself that it's a good thing.

In the end, it'll make killing him that much easier.

But as my eyes close and his scent curls around me, I can almost taste the lie on my tongue.

* * *

"You look entirely too ravishing to have been kept up all night," Tor says by way of greeting as he sits across from me at the dining hall breakfast table. His eyes fall accusingly to Steel, who sits on my right. "I'm disappointed in you, brother."

Steel ignores him, content to enjoy his bowl of creamy oats.

"Thank you?" I say, but it sounds like a question. He *did* say I look ravishing, and I can't help but agree. After a complete night's rest, a blissfully hot shower, and a simple yet elegant pair of amethyst silk pants and sleeveless top, I'm feeling more like myself than I have since boarding this ship. "I think," I add, not sure if he means it as a jab or a compliment.

"You're welcome," Tor says, winking at me as he devours a plate of eggs and meats and fruits.

Talon sits in stone silence at the head of the table, three chairs between us. He seems content to pretend I don't exist as he sips his black coffee and reads on his tablet.

"We'll be docking soon, little wife," Tor says, his tone playful. "Eat up. You'll need your energy."

I raise my brows. "Where are we docking?"

"The Air Realm," Steel answers, smoothing his hand over my thigh under the table. I gasp slightly, a swirl of heat spiraling in my core. His touch is effortless yet claiming, and I can feel the power of his endless well of strength coaxing along my skin. The ice in my blood rises, almost like an interested feline wanting to play. "We need to refuel."

"I've never been—"

"Of course, you've never been," Talon says, smacking his tablet onto the table. "You're a Shattered Isler. Your kind have no business in the elemental cities."

My chest stings at his use of *my kind*. He has no idea who my people are, how wonderful and generous they are. How much I want to free them from the fear they live in. I part my lips to say something, anything—

"She is an All Plane princess," Steel says with a calculated calm that sends chills along my skin. Tor waggles his eyebrows at the chill bumps exposed on my bare arms. "Her own Shattered Isle is the elemental city of water. If you have nothing nice to say, shut your fucking mouth, Talon."

I gape at Steel, another crash of heat soaring down the center of me with his harsh words. Since I met him he's been gentle and kind and calm, but this? He's not standing for Talon's barbing.

And I *like* it.

Fuck, I'm in trouble. Apparently, the contrast of gentle and dangerous is like my own personal weakness, because that growing ache between my thighs intensifies another degree. I could blame the desire on the bond begging for competition, but it'd be a lie.

Talon shoots Steel a bitter smile that carries the promise of pain.

I'm as shocked as anyone as I narrow my gaze at Talon, intercepting the silent threat and matching him with one of my own. His gaze shifts solely to mine, and we stare each other down with equal malice, neither of us willing to give an inch.

But I *have to* give an inch because he is technically my husband, and I shouldn't be defending Steel anyway, not with what I've been sent here to do.

Night damn me, it's only been a day, and already I'm floundering with my mission.

I relent the fight, tearing my eyes away from Talon and focusing on Tor, Steel's hand still on my thigh. "Will we get to explore the city?" I ask as if Talon's words and silent threats hold no effect on me whatsoever. "Or do we stay on board while the ship is fueled?"

Tor grins, a promise of pleasure and adventure and danger. "I'll show you the city, little wife," he says. "I'm dying to find out if you can keep up."

I can't hold back a grin. The thrill of a challenge is too much for me to keep contained.

"We will *all* accompany you into the Air Realm," Steel says, sliding his hand up an inch higher on my thigh. And with the silk pants I wear? I can feel the strength in his fingers, the heat from his hand searing my skin beneath the fabric. I can imagine what those fingers would feel like inside me, pumping, curling, and—

"Eat, little wife," Tor demands, drawing my attention from Steel's fiery gaze. I didn't even realize I'd turned my head and drifted dangerously close to Steel's lips.

Steel glares at his brother across the table, but Tor merely laughs.

And me? I do as I'm told, because truly, keeping up with these three will require *stores* of energy. So, I eat double my fill and then send a silent prayer to the night gods that I can maintain my heart while I play this part.

4
CARI

*B*y the time we dock in the Air Realm, my head is clear, and I have a wall of ice around my heart. I've used the time it took to change into a more weather-appropriate long sleeve—electing to stick with the silk trousers—to remind myself of every grievance the princes' people have done to mine.

Centuries of war between our realms.

The All Plane warriors wiping out entire cities of ours because we don't worship the sun like they do. Not to mention the sequestering of our realm, while also never assisting in aid when other realms challenged us.

At least, in that, we'd survived. No other realm, except for the All Plane, had posed a *genuine* challenge to us. And few have tried since to defy my father, but still. The All Plane king and his warriors have attacked us unprovoked too many times to count.

And I'm now married to his sons.

Married to princes who walk ahead of me now, out of the ship, and into the bright sun. It lights up a crystal blue sky stretching over a bustling city that sparkles like diamonds.

My breath catches at the sight of intricately placed buildings whose tops tickle the fluffy white clouds. Countless people stroll along elegantly crafted streets in the sky—a succession of bridges hoisted in tiers, each one higher than the next.

Of course, I expected nothing less from the Air Realm, but still marvel at the display in the elemental power as several people wield the wind to their advantage, moving items in their shops along the bridges or playing games by tossing balls of wind back and forth.

We climb onto the first available bridge, eying the endless rows of venders offering weapons and wares, clothing and tonics, treats and consumables. The smells are enticing as we climb higher, the air sweet and spicy and sharp.

Father had sent me to many of our outer cities before to handle traitors or remind rebellious villages to not bite the hand that feeds them, but I've never seen anything like this before. The energy of the Air Realm is infectious, joyous even.

"What do you think, little wife?" Tor asks me, glancing over his shoulder to look down at me.

"It's beautiful," I admit. There is no need to lie. I may have reminded myself how each of these males is my enemy, but I still have a role to play. Still have their trust to earn.

"Not as beautiful as you," Steel whispers in my ear, his hand smoothing over the small of my back. Warm chills race over my skin, and I hate that my heart softens at his compliment.

"These clothes suit you more than the dress, though I will gladly look at you in either."

I give him a smile because I can't help it. He's noticed my preference for the mobility of pants over frilly dresses. There is a comfort in knowing I can run or kick or leap at a moment's notice. Not that I expect an attack today, but I was raised to always be prepared.

Talon rolls his eyes, walking faster and disappearing into the crowd of patrons browsing the various vendors. I ignore him, choosing instead to delight in the vendors myself, my eyes taking in every detailed product they offer. Many are hand-crafted items, each one showing how much time and work and pride went into its creation.

And the people bow and smile at my new husbands as we walk by, most offering free wares in *thanks*.

Steel must notice my confusion after the fourteenth person has bowed to them because he leans down to my ear. "The Air Realm was overrun by Corters a few years ago," he explains, his blue eyes gazing over the bustling city. "All of this was almost ash. The Corters outnumbered them and slaughtered half of their people for spite. Even the younglings."

I gasp, glancing at the joyous faces I see. Corters held the number two spot for enemies to the Shattered Isle, just under the All Plane. Their people are a ruthless kind, always hunting for more power or land. "I didn't hear of this…"

"You wouldn't have," he says as we continue to walk, Tor quiet and contemplative as Steel tells the story. "Word likely wouldn't reach the Shattered Isle—"

"Because everyone knows about your father's lack of empathy for those in peril," Tor cuts him off.

Steel glares at him.

"You don't know my father," I snap.

"Do you?" Tor asks with rage in his eyes as he gestures toward the city. "These people were being slaughtered for no other reason than the Corters wanted their territory. Your father, being the king of the closest realm to offer aid, *refused* to respond. He's heard many calls like it in the past and never once tried to help. In fact, he's ordered—"

"*We* heard the distress call in the All Plane," Steel says over Tor's rant, and my heart is left racing at his words. Had my father truly heard calls like this and not sent our extensive armies to help? "And we answered it promptly," Steel continues. "The Air Realm people are innocent, their cities peaceful. We were the only ones to come to their defense. That's why they're behaving so gratefully toward us, even though we've told them countless times it isn't necessary."

I walk with them, but my mood was sour from Tor's words. "They should thank the warriors who bought them their freedom, not the princes who likely sat at the encampment, waiting for their soldiers to do their work for them," I say before I can stop myself.

Steel's brow furrows in confusion, but a growl rumbles in Tor's chest. He yanks me aside, navigating through crowds of people that part at the warrior's moves. He jerks me to a halt, pressing my spine up against one of those glittering buildings.

I stare up at him, no hint of submission in my eyes.

Not with him.

Sweet looks and gentle touches won't win him over like with Steel. Not this warrior with lightning in his veins.

Tor grips my shoulders, and the faintest hint of electricity crackles on my skin, making my muscles tense.

If he wants, he can send enough lightning through my body to stop my heart.

Everything in me narrows to that knowledge, my heart racing at the challenge as I stare up at him defiantly.

"*I* bled here, little wife," he growls.

"*You?*" I ask. "You fought with your warriors? A prince?"

He smirks down at me, and his grip loosens on my shoulders. "We all did," he says. "We always do. It doesn't matter that we have royal blood in our veins. We fight with our warriors because we are the strongest among them, with powers gifted to us by the sun gods."

I swallow hard, completely rattled. Father keeps his most powerful warriors confined to the palace, using them as his own personal guards. He never once let them fight with the warriors they trained, let alone sent them off to help other cities or villages in need.

"Surprised, little wife?" Tor asks, releasing me completely but making no move to back away. He stands so close his massive body nearly covers mine, and the sharp scent of fire and spice washes over me.

Night damn me, it's as intoxicating as Steel's, but totally different. And I can't stop my body from reacting to how close he stands, to the power I can feel teasing my own. The incessant ache low in my core ramps up another degree, and I'm so coiled with tension I want to snap.

Again, I can blame it on the fact that I haven't yet consummated that bonding with any of them and so the magic between us is urging me to, but it's *more* than that.

I'm attracted to these princes.

To the villains in my story.

They're not remotely close to what I expected, and that has my head spinning, my heart floundering, and my body *begging*.

"Yes," I finally admit. "I've never heard of princes fighting with their warriors."

His eyes travel over my body, studying me before he returns my gaze. A mischievous smile shapes his lips. "I'm sure I'll keep surprising you," he says, then leans down close enough that I can feel his warm breath on my cheeks. "But accuse me or my brothers of sitting on the sidelines and allowing our people to bleed for us again, and I'll punish you in ways even your Shattered Isle mind can't imagine."

A lick of flame darts through my blood at the way his tongue curls around the words, more like a seductive taunt than an actual threat. And damn it, my thighs clench as images race through my mind of just what kind of punishment he's talking about, because from the look in his eyes? It has less to do with torture and more to do with keeping me up for nights on end without a break.

A warm shiver races down my spine, and I dart my tongue out to wet my suddenly dry lips. Tor tracks the move with a warrior's focus, and he shifts, resting one of his bulging arms on either side of my head, caging me in.

I hold my breath, my heart racing as we watch each other, wondering who will break first. Because I can see what he wants, can practically feel his need to claim me crackling between us like his lightning did a moment ago.

"Your highness," a passerby says, bowing deep at the waist as she carries a basket of packaged and dried meats. "I've been awaiting your return. I've made your favorite," she says, and Tor's demeanor instantly shifts as he shoves off the wall and turns to face the Air Realm female.

"You spoil me," he says, a genuine smile replacing the taunting one from before. The female beams at him, a familiarity passing between them that has heat thrashing in my stomach.

Wait, what?

I can*not* be jealous of this female.

Who cares if he's all smiles and boisterous laughter as he follows her down the alleyway, talking and laughing like they're the oldest of friends? I'm here to kill him and his brothers.

Then why is your stomach twisting?

Good fucking question. Sure, Steel has been kind and inviting, and maybe my heart beat for him for a moment, but Tor? He's a brute. And *Talon*. At least he treats me as he should—as an enemy.

"Come, wife," Steel calls to me from the opening of the alleyway. "Let's spoil *you*."

I shift my features as quickly as possible, sliding my hand into his as he guides me from booth to booth, buying more gifts than I'll ever need, but explaining he only does so to support the people of the realm.

And I *hate* that my mind whirls with questions with each person we pass. Each grateful and adoring fan of my new husbands, looking at them like they're the saviors of the story and not the monsters I've been told they are.

I hate it even more that I can't stop the sinking feeling in my gut, the doubt filling me like the seeds of a weed planted in my heart. It would be easier if they'd outright tortured me when I arrived. Thrown me in a cell and used my body for whatever they wished. At least then there would be no doubts about their depravity.

But how can they be the villains from the stories I grew up with, if they've bled to save a realm that isn't their own?

* * *

Steel, Tor, and Talon—who returned to our group an hour ago—are caught up in a deep conversation with a weapons vendor, so I decide to wander, exploring the views from the bridge that wraps around the highest point of the glittering building.

The air is thin this far up, and I can feel the effects in my lungs. It's like they can't stretch wide enough or draw in enough air, so I pace myself as I walk around the bridge, exploring the opposite side. The people of this realm smile and nod as I pass, and I know it has more to do with their genuine goodness rather than my association with the princes. These people are hopeful and joyous, and it's a refreshing change when even my home can be bleak and weary on any given day.

I pause to admire the view, noting the sky shifting from its once crystal blue to a now deep indigo. The clouds are now wisps of pink and lavender, casting the sky in a smear of color that suits the lightness of the Air Realm.

After a while, I continue along my walk, intending to circle back to where I left Steel and Tor and Talon. With the sun setting, vendors are packing up their wares, locking up their boxes of goods and heading to the lower levels where food is served.

Turning a corner, I wonder if the weapons conversation has been settled or if the princes are still—

I'm jerked backward as a firm hand slides around my waist, hauling my spine against a hard chest. I struggle against the grasp until I feel an icy blade at the base of my throat. I'm dragged down a vacant bridge cast in the shadows of the two sky buildings.

My heart races against my chest, my ice power spiraling in my palms, but the knife at my throat keeps me from releasing it. Its sharp edge presses so firm against my skin that I struggle to even swallow.

"The city hasn't stopped whispering about you since you arrived," a male voice says, his lips grazing the shell of my ear.

Something inside me stirs, a searing heat I can't explain.

"You're the princes' new plaything," he continues, and I snap my hands up, gripping the powerful arm encased around my chest. "Ah ah," he says, digging the blade in a bit deeper. I hiss at the slight sting, my body arching backward in an attempt to get as far away from the burn as possible.

A low groan sounds from the male, the deep rumble vibrating from his chest directly onto my back.

"How much torment I'll be able to inflict upon them," he says. "Now that I have their bride." He presses his cheek against my temple, ensuring there is no part of our bodies that isn't touching.

And that heat inside me unfurls, grows, *blazes*.

What. The. Fuck.

I draw my power into my palms, demanding my body to comply to *me*, but before my ice can kiss his skin—

The Air Realm bridge, shadowed and vacant, *dissolves*. The shift is so jarring, I tremble against my captor as black bleeds over my vision.

I slam onto a wooden chair so hard my teeth rattle. My hands and feet are instantly bound with ropes tight enough to numb my limbs. I scan the area, searching for an exit, or at least a weapon, but there is nothing but darkness.

"Were you sent here?" The male voice is everywhere at once, and I can feel the kiss of his blade once again at my neck.

I shake my head, refusing to answer.

How did I get here? How did I get from the bridge to… wherever this is?

Think. Work the problem. Escape.

I draw in a deep breath, forcing the panic and adrenaline in my veins to calm. The key to survival in any attack is never surrendering to fear.

Something curls against my mind, a gentle warmth that feels foreign and yet inviting at the same time. Almost like—

"Cari!" Steel's voice cracks through the surrounding space, and my ears pop.

My vision clears.

I'm still pressed against my captor, his knife still poised at my neck.

Steel and Tor are rushing toward me, Talon not far behind them.

"Brother," Tor growls, white-hot lightning crackling in his eyes. "Release her."

Brother?

Ice skates down my spine.

"Lock," I whisper, the motion causing that knife to scrape against my skin.

"Say it again," he says in my ear.

"Let her go," Steel demands, and I can feel Lock smile where his cheek is pressed against my temple.

"But she feels like mine," Lock says.

My stomach flips at his words, my insides a battle between the instincts of my position and the instincts of our bond. He's an All Plane prince, and therefore, I am bound to him, too.

Fuck my life.

"Lock," Talon finally speaks up, and I half wonder if he's going to order Lock to kill me. "What are you doing here?"

The pressure of the blade at my throat eases a fraction, but his hold around my waist doesn't. "You know how much I love the elemental realms," he says, and my eyes lock on Steel's, who looks ready to rip his own brother's head off if he doesn't let me go.

Ice fills my palms to frost over Lock's hold. He hisses, jerking back from me with a laugh.

"That was harsh, darling," he says, but I barely hear him because Steel's arms are instantly around me, hauling me away from Lock.

I spin around, trying to look at him, but Talon and Tor are herding him into a corner, and all I can see are his hands raised in submission before Steel whisks me around the corner.

"Are you hurt?" he asks, his voice frantic as he walks us down the building and toward the ship with an unmatched speed fueled by his power. He's so fast it makes my head spin.

"No," I assure him. "He took me by surprise, that's all."

"He's lucky then," Steel says once we reach the ship. "Because he'd be dead if he'd harmed you."

I shudder at the promise in those words, and draw in a long breath once Steel finally stops outside my bedchamber. I look up at him, noting the genuine concern in his eyes. I reach up a hand and smooth it over his hard jaw.

"I'm fine," I say. "What will they to do to him?"

Steel leans into my touch, cocking a brow at me. "You sound worried."

I swallow hard. How can I be worried about someone who just had a knife to my throat? How can I be worried about the estranged, traitorous prince of the All Plane?

5
TALON

"Finally decide to release me from my cage, brother?" Lock steps up to the glass containing his chamber, and I roll my eyes.

"You have a cell big enough to house a small home, plus all the luxuries you could ever want," I say, eying the plush furniture decorating his lounge area and the massive obsidian bed beyond. "I'd hardly call it a cage. And after you attacked Steel's princess, you should be grateful you're even alive," I add, shaking my head. It's been two days since he grabbed Cari at the Air Realm, and I still haven't figured out *why* he did it. We weren't even on his trail, so why expose himself now?

His dark eyes narrow on me, but I turn around, focusing on my target across the hall from him.

"I can't come and go freely," Lock says as I fiddle with the control panel on the opposite wall.

A maintenance alert pinged me this morning, and now seems like the perfect time to fix it. Much better than breakfasting with Steel and Tor and watching them fawn over Cari every five seconds. I'd only been able to handle a few minutes of those nauseating exchanges before heading down here.

"So a cage it is," Lock continues, and I lower the tool in my hand, turning around. I lean against the wall, folding my arms over my chest.

"You're the one who waged war on Father," I say, not that I can totally blame him. Father can be a real dick sometimes, but to outright defy him? No one has been stupid enough to do that beyond the Shattered Isle king and Lock.

Lock smirks, pacing the length of the floor-to-ceiling glass doors of his containment chamber. His long hunter-green jacket hovers just above the floor, his boots near silent against the tiles. "I wouldn't call it war," he says, shrugging. "More of a defiance against utter bullshit and injustice."

I laugh because I can't help it.

"I've missed you," I admit. We'd been chasing him for over a year. Practically *hunting* him after he'd stolen some vital plans from father and disappeared. He still hasn't told us what was on those plans that had been worth getting banished over, but then again, Lock has always been the most mischievous and rebellious of us all.

I turn around when he doesn't return my sentiment, continuing to fix the panel in a weighted silence. Tor and I have discussed it many times with Steel over the last two days... we don't know what Father will do when we bring Lock home. My money is on publicly executing him, which doesn't sit right with me.

A lot of things haven't been sitting right with me with Father's decisions lately—including marrying us off to a

Shattered Isler—but outright saying so will result in my imprisonment too. I need more time to think, to strategize. And that's the only good thing to come out of this ridiculous joke of a marriage—the time this journey will give me to formulate a solid plan.

One that hopefully saves my brother, not that I'll ever admit that to him.

"You seem out of sorts," Lock says, and I shut the panel, having too-easily fixed the minor mechanical issue. I'm desperate for a more extensive project. Something like an engine failing would probably bring me the distraction I need, but I'm not about to sabotage the ship to soothe my overcrowded mind. "Even your tinkering seems dull. What is it?"

"Can't you conjure something else to entertain you?" I ask, but the jab is half-hearted.

He pauses as I step up to the glass separating us. "Would you rather I take a peek inside *your* head?" he asks, his tone level. "What can I possibly conjure that will be half as fun as that?"

"Don't," I warn. We've had an ironclad agreement since we were kids—we never use our powers against each other. Though Steel and Tor seemed damn close to breaking that vow when Lock had their precious Cari under his blade.

We'd struck the oath after a horrendous year of fighting with each other—Lock, with his conjuring and enchantment powers, had been the worst in all of it. That summer he'd made each of us live out our worst fears, despite keeping us safely locked in our rooms. Tor had returned the favor with the full force of his lightning powers. Steel had pummeled him with his sheer strength. And me? Well, I'd created a host of indestructible robots that prevented him from falling asleep for weeks on end.

We nearly killed each other until we finally called a truce. None of us would ever truly murder the other, so we agreed to never use our powers against each other again.

"You're no fun," he teases, and continues his pacing. "Married life isn't all it's cracked up to be?" he asks, and I cock a brow at him.

He shrugs again, shifting some of his long black hair off his shoulders. "Just because I don't peek in your minds doesn't mean I can't see into the staffs'."

"What do they think of her?" I ask.

"They adore her," he says. "And who wouldn't? Those legs go on for days, and her eyes?" He closes his for a moment, inhaling deeply as if he's savoring some memory I can't possibly understand. "Not to mention she's learned all their names and graciously thanks them every time they tend to her."

"I can't stand her," I say, anger burning my chest.

Lock's eyes snap open, and he tilts his head. "Brother, you can't—"

"Is she gorgeous? Yes." I'm not blind. Did the bonding ceremony make me want to bend her over my work station and fuck her until she can't walk straight? Yes. "But she's our enemy," I say, almost like I'm trying to convince myself.

Lock narrows his gaze at me. "By what definition?"

"She's of the Shattered Isle," I say. "And not some random city within the realm that can't be held accountable for their king's actions. She's the king's *daughter*. Raised by the very person who robbed us of our mother."

"Ah," he says, nodding. Something like sadness flickers in his gaze, but it's gone a blink later.

"She also has expressed her clear dislike and distrust for our realm, our father—"

"By those standards," he cuts me off. "You can say I'm your enemy, too." I look at him pointedly, and he laughs again. "Come now, brother. You can't honestly say you want to see my head on Father's chopping block?" Something like doubt colors his features, but he quickly smooths them.

I clear my throat, hating the sudden tightness there. "I don't know what Father will do to you."

Lock slams a fist on the glass, and I reach for the weapon holstered at my side. One of my own making, able to slice through any material, no matter how strong or thick.

"You know exactly what he'll do to me," he says, his voice low, lethal—the voice of the Lock in the rumors that have spread across the realms. The villain of the All Plane, the traitor to his throne.

But *I* look at him and see my baby brother. The same boy I used to create toys for when Father would lock him in his room for weeks on end for arguing during his history lessons or for sneaking out after dark, just to watch the stars.

Stargazing is frowned upon in our culture. Father proclaimed the stars held power to steal our minds, to warp them into the ways of the Shattered Islers. But Lock could never resist the draw they had on him, and Father delighted in punishing him for it. It's no wonder Lock went up against him the minute he was powerful enough to do so. If he wanted, he could've ended my father then and there. Made him believe he was drowning until his body succumbed to the mental panic.

But he didn't.

And it kept me up nights wondering *why*.

"Steel is already smitten with her," I say, desperate to change the subject.

"Of course, he is," Lock says, lowering his fist and relaxing his shoulders. "He's always had the biggest heart among us."

I nod.

"And Tor?" he asks.

I shrug. "I think he sees her more as a challenge than anything. Unexplored terrain and all that."

Lock snorts. "If she can survive a night with him, maybe she's worth the fuss."

I agree, but don't say as much.

"And you hate her, just because of where and who she was born to."

I swallow the acid in my throat. When he says it like that, I sound like a grade-A asshole. But how can I get past the history between our realms?

She has.

Or has she? I counter that voice deep in my mind. "What if she's here to betray us?" I pose the question aloud. I wouldn't put it past the Shattered Isle king to agree to this union simply to send a viper into our realm. A beautiful viper, I'll give her that. Maybe that's part of it. A pretty, distracting package that will poison us the second we drop our guard.

"What if the kings want a peaceful solution to our terrible history?" Lock asks.

I give him an incredulous look. "Do you truly believe that, brother? With your hatred of both kings?"

He shrugs again, stalking to the chaise lounge in the corner—one of his own conjuring—and drops into it. All the items in his chamber he conjured seconds after we'd thrown him inside it. He extends his arms over the back of the lounge, stretching wide as he smirks up at me. "I have a solution to your problem."

"Oh, you do, do you?" I almost laugh.

"Put the female in here with me," he says, his dark eyes bordering on the madness he's never entirely kept at bay. "One night with me, and I'll give you everything you need to know about her. I've already slipped inside her mind once. I can do it again, and you'll know without a doubt if you can trust our darling wife or not."

Tempting.

Extremely tempting.

Especially with each time she mouths off at me or tries to protect Steel—like I'd harm my own damn brother. "So, you're saying I can trust your word?" I ask, and the joke hurts more than it should. I haven't seen my brother in over a year, and the wreckage that he's left behind? How am I supposed to forget all of that and believe him?

Too many questions.

Too many secrets.

For once, I envy his power. The ability to slip into others' minds and find out their intentions. I'd love to use it on him and Cari right now.

"What do you think, brother?" he asks, a grim smile on his face. He shows no signs of hurt at my distrust.

"I think..." I say, sighing. I don't have the answers right now, and I've never been good at living with unsolved problems. I glance out the window down the hall, noting the sun setting in the cobalt sky. "It's a tempting offer, brother," I finally say.

Lock has given me even more to think about. I need to find something to take apart and put back together again. Fast.

"I'll let you know if I decide to take you up on it or not." I move down the hallway, not bothering to offer him a goodbye.

"I'll be here," he calls out, the annoyance in his tone not lost on me. And for a split second, the guilt of caging my brother —regardless of how pretty and comfortable the cage may be —smacks me across the face.

That containment chamber is tailored specifically to his powers. He can't conjure a key or passcode out of it, nor a weapon that can shatter the glass. I built it specifically to counteract all of that.

Me.

I'm the creator of my brother's current torment, and I hate that my power gave me the tools to do so. But I can't take chances with him. Not when he's left a string of bodies in his escape from the All Plane and is currently holding the position as the most terrifying creature across the realms—even above the damn Shattered Isle king, which is saying something.

But, I also can't deny the doubt in my mind. Lock is powerful, rebellious even, but he's never done anything without a purpose.

I rub my palms over my face as I reach my chambers, falling onto my bed with the sudden urge to sleep this entire journey away. The more Steel and Tor fall for Cari, the more I'm tempted to take Lock up on his offer.

Perhaps if I trap her in that cell with him, they'll tear each other apart and solve all my problems.

6
CARI

After two leisurely days on the ship, most of the time spent eating and drinking and getting to know Tor and Steel even more, I'm a tangled mess of nerves. And it's not because of the attack and capture of Lock from two days ago, despite my dreams being haunted by the sound of his voice in my ear.

I'm exhausted with myself, with my constant internal battles, so I retire to my room the second dinner is over, my mind and body a war of emotions that has me wound tight. Steel makes no move to follow me, and for that, I'm grateful. I know I need to complete the bonding process with each of them—it will go miles in gaining their full trust—but I'm…

Conflicted.

I lean against the smooth wall near the floor-to-ceiling window of my room. Pinpricks of diamonds sparkle in a sea of liquid black, and the sight washes over me like a comforting blanket. At least the night is my constant, even if I have to endure the sun for far longer than I ever have before. I should be asleep, shifting my hours to match the princes', but I'm restless.

Despite the stories my father has told, the history I've grown up knowing like my own blood...I'm growing *fond* of my husbands.

Not Talon, who hates me as I should hate all of them, but Steel and Tor? I can't deny the attraction I feel for both of them, the need I can feel coursing through my veins right this second. And it has me questioning *everything*.

Their history is starkly different from my own, but isn't that always the case? Don't heroes paint themselves as such and vice versa? But which version of history is true? It's hard to tell, especially after spending so much time with them, not to mention the adoring people of the Air Realm. They have no stake in my opinions of my husbands, no agenda. They simply worship the All Plane princes because they saved their realm. And the way my husbands treated them?

It was... infuriating.

Because they didn't treat them with a royal disdain toward commoners. They didn't turn their noses up at their homemade goods or spit on their shoes when they offered dinner and drinks and dancing.

They thanked them, honored them, indulged them in whatever they wanted.

They acted *nothing* like the males my father described.

I rub my hands over my bare arms, having slipped into a white silk top and shorts for bedtime. But sleep is the last thing on my mind as I slink toward the massive bed.

I sigh as I sink against its mountain of pillows and blankets, the fabric luxurious against my sensitive skin.

My father had gone so far as to say that all three males wouldn't hesitate to take me against my will, to have their way with me one after another like honorless barbarians. He said they may take their pleasure with me so much that I'd be lucky to survive a night, let alone the whole journey. And with the power each of the princes held, I knew my father was right.

At least, I'd believed him *then*.

Now?

The princes haven't even *hinted* at doing such a thing. Any one of them, with their sheer strength and power, could've forced the completion of the bonding process at any time.

But they haven't.

They haven't even punished me for speaking my mind—something my father punished me for often. Even after he'd ordered General Payne to beat my own opinions out of me, it never worked. I'd simply learned how to control my tongue around my father. But here? Without so much as a hint of punishment? I've spoken my mind, challenged Steel's stories about my people and his, and he'd met me with an open mind. Even Tor, who I'd riled up two days ago in the Air Realm, hadn't truly harmed me. Not in the way my father's general did. And I hated that I'd never questioned that treatment before now…was it not like that in all the realms? From my husbands' behavior, I very much doubted it.

And that made me feel more conflicted than ever before.

Because what did it say about my father's nature, if it wasn't common practice to beat your daughter senseless when she made a mistake in her training or spoke her mind?

I blow out a breath, my mind whirling with contradictions. And I keep circling back to the moment Tor pressed me against that building, the rage rippling off him like a thunder storm and yet, he'd leashed that rage for *me*. To keep from truly hurting me. And thinking about that has my body aching so much I toss and turn on the bed.

I try and clear my mind, letting go of each worry I have. I can't shed my ingrained hatred toward the princes and their father in the span of a few pleasant encounters. Maybe they're behaving this way for my benefit, using a strategy of their own. But even that thought doesn't ring true, especially after the past few days.

I sigh again, stretching my limbs in an attempt to rid myself of the restless energy, but it doesn't help.

And as my mind finally clears, leaving the worrying for tomorrow, the next day, every day until I uncover their true nature, all I can think about is the way Tor pressed me up against that building. The way he smelled, his power crackling over my skin.

I can practically feel Steel's hand on my thigh, teasing ever higher at breakfast this morning.

I see their smiles behind my closed eyes, smell their scents on my skin from each innocent and intoxicating touch we've shared.

The pulsing ache deepens with each breath, and I slide my hands along my body. I pretend my left hand is Steel's, delicately teasing my breasts. My right hand becomes Tor's, gliding over my stomach and slipping beneath the band of my silk shorts. I arch into my own touch, my fingers sliding through my heat, slippery from thoughts of the princes.

I sigh at the much-needed contact, my eyes shut, seeing nothing but Steel and Tor on either side of me. Their hands claiming and teasing every inch of me.

Night damn me. I dip my fingers into my heat, pumping with a strength I wish is the warriors'. I rock into the touch, all the while teasing my breasts until my nipples are peaked and aching. My mind storms with thoughts of Steel's mouth on mine, Tor's lips on my skin.

My breathing hitches, sweet release only a few seconds away—

A soft creak sends me plummeting to reality, and I freeze as my eyes snap open.

Tor stands at the foot of my bed, a smirk on his lips as his eyes drink in my position and linger on my hand buried beneath my shorts.

My heart thuds against my chest, heat blooming on my cheeks as he stretches his hands up, gripping the top bedrail where silk curtains hang from, his biceps rippling from the motion.

I shift, drawing my hand back as if that will erase what he's already seen.

"Don't you dare stop," he says, his tone primal and rough.

A lick of flame shoots down my spine, my lips parting.

He nods to my right hand, and the command in his eyes is clear.

I can say no.

I can call for Steel.

I can do anything other than listen to the fire pulsing in my veins, telling me to bend to Tor's will.

He shifts his weight, the slight move drawing my attention. He's changed into a simple pair of black pajama bottoms and a matching sleeveless top, the fabric straining against his considerable muscles, like he was carved from the sun itself. And his eyes? They're drenched in command and lust as he dares me to challenge him.

And after all the teasing, aching tension we've dealt each other recently?

I don't want to.

And from the swell I see in his pants, I can tell he feels it just as badly as I do. No doubt it's why he's ventured into my room in the middle of the night.

Why didn't I lock the door?

You know why.

Because I wanted him or Steel to come and play with me.

I hold his gaze as I slide my hand beneath my shorts again, shifting my legs wider as my fingers dip into my heat. I tremble as Tor's eyes narrow to where I touch myself, my fingers shaking as I tease my breasts, too. I rock into the touch, never once taking my eyes off him.

His muscles tense as he watches me, his eyes hooded and glazed, but he keeps his hands up and curled around that bedrail, as if it alone is holding him in place.

"Stop," he demands. I halt my fingers. He nods, a satisfied smirk on his lips. "Take your clothes off, little wife."

I hesitate for a breathless moment, then pull my shirt over my head, tossing it to the side. My breasts are full and heavy, my nipples pert from my own teasing. My shorts soon join the top, and I lean back against the pillows again, fully on display for the warrior.

Lightning crackles in his eyes as he drinks me in, and I feel the heat of his gaze like a brand. Every inch of me is coiled tight with need, the ache between my thighs so deep now I can hardly breathe around it.

"Fuck," he says on a released breath. "You're stunning." He nods again. "Continue."

The word is both a demand and a release, and I plunge my hand between my thighs. I'm desperate for this to last as long as possible while at the same time I'm hungry for the relief to this incessant ache.

His eyes track every touch, every move, with a warrior's focus. He smirks, wets his lips, but he makes no move to join me. And maybe it's because I haven't given him an invitation, but I'm terrified to say anything. I don't want this game to end, and I have no clue what that says about me, about the mission I'm on, but right now? I don't fucking care. Nothing exists outside of this need pulsing between us.

I up my pace, dipping in harder and deeper, knowing exactly what I need to make myself come. I lift my hips off the bed, using the momentum and pretending all the while it's Tor's body I'm crashing against. And with him standing right there? Watching me with lightning in his eyes? It's not a difficult fantasy to conjure.

My thighs clench, and I tip my head back, ready for the last stroke to send me soaring over that sweet edge—

Lightning snaps in the room, and a soft pop sounds as a bolt of it encircles my wrist, drawing it away from my slick heat and securing it above my head. A blink later, and my other wrist is secured there too, the bands of lightning buzzing against my skin with a pleasant burn.

Tor releases his grip on the bedrail, tugging his shirt over his head and dropping his pants just as quickly.

My mouth goes dry at the sight of him. His chest and abdomen are pure, carved muscle, decorated with different battle scars that only amplify how strong he is, how much he's survived—further shattering my assumption that the princes didn't fight with their soldiers. My gaze trails lower, over his delicious V-lines, his massive thighs, and the sheer size of his hard cock.

"Tell me you weren't picturing me just now, little wife," he says, and my eyes snap back up to his. He kneels on the bed, his hands hovering above my ankles.

I tug slightly at my bonds, and I'm met with a ripple of pain that trembles down my spine, making me gasp. He smirks down at me, an eyebrow cocked as he waits for my answer. The words are caught in my throat, my body a humming string of need. His lightning ropes are a mixture of pain and pleasure, only making me want him more.

"Tell me you don't want me," he says, his voice rough as he fists his hard cock in one hand. I nearly whimper at the sight, at the pure confidence in his eyes as he pumps himself in front of me. "And I'll leave right now."

Shock rattles through me, and he notes the surprise in my eyes, smirking.

My breath catches, and I tug on the bonds again, my hands desperate to touch him or touch myself, anything to slake the need pulsing between my thighs. Another shiver of pain races over my skin, and I gasp. "Yes!"

Tor stills, tilting his head. "Yes, what?"

"I pictured you," I admit. "You and Steel."

A slow, seductive smile curls his lips as he stops pumping himself. He shifts his knees on the bed, parting my thighs with his powerful hands, and dips his head low enough that I can feel the heat of his breath on my pussy.

I look down my body at him, my hands still secured above my head. Night damn me, the sight of him there is nearly enough to make me come.

"Soon," he says, and I shiver with the warmth of his breath washing over me. "My brother and I will worship you." He darts his tongue out, a too-light tease over my swollen flesh. "But tonight?" he continues. "I want you all to myself." He dips his head, and I arch into his mouth. A gasp rips from my lips at the feel of him against me.

His tongue. Holy fuck, his *tongue*.

He plunges it inside me. No more teasing flicks. He *claims* me, lapping at me as he grips my thighs, shifting me until my knees are over his broad shoulders and he's devouring me from a deeper angle. I rock into him, totally abandoning myself to the sensations he draws from me, giving in to pure instinct as I seek more and more from him.

He growls against me, the vibrations from his mouth sparking that swollen bundle of nerves until I shatter completely around him. I bow off the bed, and his hands shift under my ass, holding me up against him, not letting me back off an inch as he eats at me relentlessly, sending one orgasm right into another until my muscles are limp, and he and his lightning bonds are the only thing holding me up.

"Fuck," he growls, drawing back enough to look up at me. "You're delicious," he says. "I could eat your sweet pussy for hours."

I tremble at his words, the shocks from what he's already done to me still shaking my body. He lowers me to the bed, gently removing my legs from his shoulders as he kneels again. His eyes are pure mischief as he trails his fingers over my breasts, circling a pert nipple before going lower.

"From watching you," he says, dipping a finger through the slickness between my thighs. "I know you enjoy this." He teases my clit before plunging into my heat, only to draw out and come back with two fingers. He pumps inside me, and I'm instantly liquid again, my hips lifting off the bed to meet his fingers. "Am I right, little wife?" he asks, and I nod, eyes closed as I'm lost to the way he's winding me up again. "Answer me," he demands, the voice of a commander, a warrior used to getting what he wants.

"Yes," I say on a loosed breath. "Yes, I like that."

He continues to pump those strong fingers inside me, shifting until he's hovering over me. "Like?" He scoffs and sinks his mouth over one of my breasts. His teeth tease my nipple, his tongue flicking out to soothe the bite as I gasp. "I guess it'll take more to get you to say you *love* it."

It.

What he's doing to me.

Not *him*.

That's the only thing that keeps ice water from pouring all over my steamy-as-hell moment.

"Look at me," he demands, and my eyes snap open, locking on his gaze. His mouth is inches from mine, his hand still working me up and sending me catapulting toward that edge again.

Fuck, how can he feel this good? No one has ever been able to make me come this many times, and he's only used his mouth and hands. What will it feel like when he uses his cock?

Everything in me thrills at the thought, right alongside another release that shakes my entire body as he flattens the heel of his hand against my clit. He slants his mouth over mine, drinking in my moans as if he wants to taste my screams on his tongue. He tastes like pure electricity and it sends me spiraling into orbit.

He grins against my mouth, breaking our kiss as he gently pulls his fingers from me. He draws them to his mouth and sucks my flavor off of them. Apparently, he didn't get enough with the first round, and the sight of his glazed eyes as he tastes me again? It turns me into something completely primal, and there is only one thing I want.

"Release me," I demand more than ask, and he cocks a brow at me, his eyes delighted with my tone.

"When I'm ready," he challenges.

I nip at his bottom lip, catching it in my teeth and biting hard enough to hurt.

He growls, but lightning flickers in his eyes.

"Release me," I say again. "Or I'll do it myself."

Shock joins the electricity in his eyes, and he tips his chin, just a fraction. "Do it," he dares.

He wants me to. This warrior husband of mine wants me to *prove* that I can not only keep up with him, but that I'm strong enough, worthy enough of his time.

He has no idea who he's dealing with.

I grin, harnessing the power inside me gifted to me by the stars. Ice trickles from my veins, curling around the lightning bonds around my wrists, freezing the power there until all it takes is one good tug, and it crumbles like stardust on the bed.

Tor's eyes widen at the display in power, and I think it's his shock that allows me to push him off of me until his spine kisses the mattress. I straddle him, both my chilled hands pressed against his massive, muscled chest. My hair tumbles around me as I look down at him.

"I want to touch you," I say, gliding my hands over his shoulders, his chest, his abdomen. "Do I need to bind you now, husband?" I tease, and he shakes his head, clarity and lust taking away the shock in his eyes.

"Good," I say, teasing his hard-as-granite cock with the wetness between my thighs. The move sends tremors up my spine and I have to take a deep breath to continue talking. "Because ice is a bit more painful than your lightning."

He barks a laugh, the sound deep and delightful. He grabs my hips, taking the reins and rocking me harder over his considerable length. "That was for your benefit, little wife. If you want it to hurt next time, just ask," he says, his tone ragged.

I dig my fingers into the muscles on his chest, my eyes shuttering closed as he continues to guide me over him, teasing and rocking until I'm breathless with need again. Somehow, I regain a hint of focus, and grip his hands on my hips. He *lets* me draw them to my breasts, and I leave them there as I shift above him.

He goes still as I situate myself over the head of his cock, pausing there as I look down at him. Gone are the demands, the banter, the teasing. There is nothing in his eyes but pure anticipation. The weight of what this means is clear in his cobalt blue eyes.

I'm accepting our bond.

Completing our bonding ceremony.

And I don't take a second to examine that swelling feeling in my chest. Don't waste one breath agonizing over the conflict roaring in my heart.

I ignore everything but the feel of him as I sink atop him, taking him in inch by glorious inch until I'm seated to the hilt.

I blow out a breath, my body trembling as I adjust to the sheer size of him. And he doesn't press. Instead, he rolls my breasts in his hands, lightly pinching my nipples before smoothing one hand down over my stomach, my hip, and back up again. Stroking me, almost tenderly, as if he knows how much time I need to adjust.

But he's already given me so many orgasms tonight that I don't need too much of it, and I roll my hips.

He groans, his hands still roaming over my body as I move atop him.

Each time I rock against him, another wave of heat crashes inside me.

I lift up, nearly pulling him all the way out before sinking atop him again, fast and hard and needy.

He growls, a deep rumble in his chest that only begs me to do it again.

So I do.

Again and again.

I ride him, hard and frantic until I can feel that bond between us like a glowing ember in the darkness. It's a braid of power, his and mine, curling and coiling with each other until I can't tell where his starts and mine ends.

Until I can *feel* his lightning dancing with the ice in my veins.

Until it shines in my eyes and an icy breath flows past his lips.

I rock against him, relishing the feel of him inside me—his power and his cock, both working together to tie me into delicious knots. His grip on my hips tightens and he thrusts upward off the bed, driving into me from below as I take him in over and over again.

I shatter.

I unravel.

I splinter into a million pieces of light as brilliant as the stars outside.

Tor shifts beneath me, hauling upward until we're chest to chest, and he's drinking in my moans as he finds his own release inside me, a deep growl radiating between my lips as he comes.

Our breaths are matched as he draws his mouth away from mine, our chests heaving against each other as he holds me. The bond between us practically purrs as it curls up and settles happily inside me. I drop my forehead against his shoulder, delightfully exhausted.

And then he's laughing, a hearty warrior's laugh, the motion doing things to my already limp and sated body. I draw back to look at him, wonder in my eyes.

"We're just getting started, little wife," he says, and my eyes flare wide.

How much more can I take?

He flips us then, and I can feel him hardening inside me yet again as he presses me back into the bed. "Say when," he whispers against my neck before planting kisses down it.

I close my eyes, arching into him, and I don't say a fucking word.

7
TOR

"If that bountiful spread is for our little wife," I say, eying the tray Steel has piled high with fruits and pastries next to a carafe of coffee and two empty mugs. "Then you ought to let her sleep in." I can't stop running my fingers over my lips. I can still taste Cari on my tongue, and that knowledge alone makes me harden, as if I hadn't just fucked her senseless all night.

And by the sun, she's amazing. Better than I ever thought and stronger than I ever suspected. Sure, I enjoy her challenging mouth, even when she flew off the cuff the other day and insinuated that my brothers and I didn't bleed with our own armies. But she didn't know any better. We would help her see the truth.

Steel sets the tray down on the counter in the dining hall a bit loudly. "What did you do to her?"

I bark a laugh. "What *didn't* I do to her would be the more proper question, brother."

A muscle in Steel's jaw ticks, and I reel in my laughter. Can he truly blame me, though?

Not only did I just have the best sex of my entire life—and I've had plenty to compare it to—but we completed our bonding. She runs through my veins as steady as my own blood now. I can feel her sleeping all the way in her chambers, just as easily as I can feel her delicious powers of ice slumbering contently under her skin.

Who knew we'd be so lucky to be blessed with such a powerful wife? Information on the Shattered Isle king's only daughter was scarce, so we never suspected this.

"Tor," Steel warns, and I grab a large mug off the counter, pouring it to the brim with black coffee. I take a fast sip, giving him an apologetic look.

"Don't be angry with me, brother," I say, and Steel folds his arms over his chest. He's already dressed for the day in a blue, tight-fitting long-sleeve shirt and black pants.

It's only dawn, the sun barely chasing away the night. I'd left our little wife sleeping soundly only an hour ago, having kept her up all night. But, to be fair, she kept me up just as long. A thrill rushes straight to my cock at the memory of her mounting me, taking control like she could match me in strength if I pressed.

"I'm not," he admits with a sigh.

And I see it there.

"You don't need to be jealous either," I say, and he flashes me a glare. It's All Plane custom for princes to claim *one* bride, bonding with her as a connection to strengthen our own.

"I know," he says. "But you've completed the bonding process. She told me she wanted to wait…"

I clap him on the shoulder with my free hand and then quickly dart back when he tries to throw me off. I raise my hands again, one firmly gripping my mug. "I didn't intend to!" I tell him, and he slows his advance. Steel is the most level-headed out of all of us, but when he wants a fight? Sun gods be with whoever is his target. His inherit power is sheer strength, making him admittedly the strongest and fastest among us.

"Explain."

No room for argument then. I sidestep, then fall into one of the dining hall's many chairs, setting my coffee on the table.

"I went to speak with her last night," I say, lightning singing in my veins at the memory of how I found her. I shift in my chair, a deep ache wrenching in my chest. Gods, I'd had her on my tongue not an hour ago. How can I possibly already want more?

"Why?"

I blink out of the memory, forcing myself to focus. "After our spat in the market, and after having two days to calm down, I wanted to further explain my reaction." I'd lost my temper, which I'm prone to do, especially when my honor is questioned.

"How noble of you," Steel says, sinking into the chair opposite mine.

I flip him off. "I shouldn't have lost my temper," I explain. "Not with her. Not with someone who's been hand-fed lies her entire life."

At that, Steel nods his agreement. He flattens his palm on the smooth table. "It will take time," he says, "to unweave the deceit that's been spun in her mind." He sighs, and I nod as he arches a brow at me. "Did you two talk?"

I press my lips together, trying like hell to contain my grin.

Steel groans, rolling his eyes. He makes to shove away from the table, but I stop him.

"I didn't get the chance," I explain, and he remains in his seat. "She was pleasuring herself when I walked in."

Fire dances in Steel's eyes, and I lean back in my seat. "What would you have done, brother?" I ask.

He opens his mouth as if he'll say he would've left her to it, but shuts them before he can utter the lie. Again, his jaw flexes, that palm on the table curling into a fist. It's not *me* personally he's jealous of, but the act itself. He wants to be bonded to our little wife as much as me, and I'd be lying if I said we weren't all competitive.

"She's not a game," I say, and Steel snaps his eyes to mine.

"I know that," he growls. "I've never seen her that way."

"I know," I say. "And you should know, brother," I say, leaning far over the table and lowering my voice. "When I asked her if she was picturing my hands on her when she touched herself?" His glare deepens, but I continue. "She said yes."

Steel falls back in his chair, looking like he wants to punch the smirk off my face.

"But," I hurry to continue, "she said she was picturing yours on her, too."

Steel tilts his head, threatening me with a look that promises pain if I'm fucking with him.

"On my honor," I say, laying a hand over my chest. His shoulders loosen at that, knowing full well I'd never lie to him like that.

It takes a few moments, but soon, a smirk shapes his lips, and I can see the wheels turning behind his eyes, see them darken with the need to complete their bond too.

And there isn't a flicker of jealousy at the thought of them together. She's *ours*. Whether or not Talon likes it, she belongs to me, to Steel, to Talon, and fuck, even to Lock. And from the way she behaved last night? I know there is plenty of her to go around. The female has a heart big enough for each of us, but just because she gave her body to me doesn't mean we're any closer to that trust that is so desperately needed between partners.

No. I'm certain that will take much longer to achieve.

But in the meantime?

It'll sure as hell be fun for my brothers and me to make her body sing while her heart decides.

8

CARI

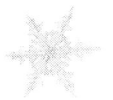

Last night changed things.

I can't explain it, but something shifted inside me I can't ignore.

Wandering the ship, I'm happy I don't run into any of the brothers at the moment. I awoke alone, took a hot shower, and delighted at the delicious soreness between my thighs. Though I'm drawn to the dining hall—where I can *feel* Tor, thanks to our bonding being complete—I hurry the opposite direction, content to explore the ship on my own and sort out my mind.

Tor's mouth on my skin, his hands hauling me against him, his lightning bonds securing me in the most incredible way...

I groan, cursing my mind. I can't stop thinking about what happened between us. Not only the sex, which was mind-blowing, but the *bonding.* He's in my blood now, a comforting humming in my heart, a beacon broadcasting where he is now, how his mood is content, excited.

Can he feel me now too? This side effect of the bond has never been explained to me. Is that because *true* bonding is so rare and intimate no written history is kept on it?

Sure, I've heard of simple pairings that don't join powers, but I've also been told of the *true bonding*, which is usually reserved for the best matches between partners. Royalty, especially. Still, why didn't father warn me of this? Because if Tor can sense my emotions, then he'll no doubt be able to tell how conflicted I am inside. But, to be fair, I can tell he's excited, but I don't know *why* he's excited, so maybe that counts for something.

I turn down another long corridor, not really taking in the luxurious sky ship as much as I wish. Bonding aside, I'm even more conflicted now than I was before the events in the Air Realm. I have no solid proof that my new husbands are monsters.

But just because I don't have proof doesn't mean they're not.

Tor didn't behave like a monster last night.

I shake off the thought, but it settles inside me. Right next to the knowledge of Steel's kindness, his perceptiveness.

I blow out a breath, forcing myself to remember the warrior I am. I control ice and water, and the dark sea calls to me under the stars. I will not be rendered useless because of one fantastic night of fucking.

A warm shiver dances along my spine, a deep craving pulsing in the center of me. Night damn me, I want more. And Tor had kept me up the entire night, that starry sky teasing me beyond the windows.

I force the memory away, centering myself with a list of tasks.

First, reside myself to uncovering evidence of them being who my father portrayed them as.

Second, continue gaining their trust.

Third, enjoy it while I can.

Because if I find evidence against them?

All goes according to plan and my daggers find a home in each of their throats.

My stomach churns so hard I pause, sliding my hand along it. The idea of hurting Steel or Tor is quickly becoming revolting. At least with Talon's hatred it's easier to picture.

And if I don't find evidence against them?

If they continue to behave as they have been?

Then what?

I shake my head, not bothering to add that resolution to my list. Because I have no idea what I'll do if they don't turn out to be the villains I've always expected them to be.

"Are you lost, darling?" a familiar deep voice calls to me from across the hall.

I straighten, coming fully around the corner of the long hallway, and freeze before a massive glass…

Cage.

I have no other way to describe it. Because despite the luxurious furniture decorating the spacious room, nothing but glass walls seal it. A control panel with multi-colored lights flash on the outside of the exterior glass wall, and I furrow my brow as I step closer to it.

A fist slams against the glass, and I stumble backward. Smoke curls around his frame, wafting off him as if he just manifested from the shadows.

Lock.

The estranged, traitorous prince who held a knife to my throat a few days ago. I didn't get a good look at him then, but now?

He's the most attractive male I've ever seen, and when I'm currently married to three other All Plane princes? That's saying something. He's so damn tall, and a long hunter-green jacket hangs off his muscled frame. A black shirt strains against his broad chest, and his hair is midnight silk brushing his shoulders. He tilts his head, examining me the way I am him, and those eyes…

Fuck, they're a crystal blue-green that changes depending on which way he's looking at me. And they're boundless, deep, and see right through the heart of me.

"You *are* lost," he says, and his deep tenor rakes over me like a caress. He drops his fist from the glass, folding his arms behind his back as he continues to stare at me.

"I'm…" I glance around, realizing he's right. I have no idea where I am, and knowing that his brothers locked him up after his capture, I know I'm not supposed to be down here.

"Yes," I admit, swallowing hard. I search for the outrage, for accusations to throw at him after he held a knife to my throat, after he conjured an illusion in my mind, but I can't find anything but…

Intrigue.

Something deep inside me flickers to life in his presence, not unlike when Tor or Steel are in the room, and I curse inwardly at the sensation.

A half-smile turns his lips up, and suddenly I can't look away from them, can't stop picturing what those lips could do if he's unleashed.

Fuck, what is *wrong* with me? Did last night unhinge some solidarity in my mind? Why else would my skin heat from just the sight of him?

Something inside me flares to life, a silent call I can't ignore, begging me to draw closer to the glass. And I *do*. I step close enough to touch it, and I can't help but reach up and trace the hard line of his jaw over the glass.

Surprise flickers over his features, but in a blink, it's gone. He looks down at me with wide eyes.

"Not used to people stepping so close to your cage?" I boldly ask, dropping my hand.

"Most are too afraid to get close to me," he says, and again, his damn voice makes my breath catch. Chills raise over my skin, and an ache wrenches deep inside me. It's like I know him, even though we only shared a moment in time together.

"Hmm," I say instead of voicing my rising panic. I can't possibly be drawn to the male who intended to kidnap me the other day. To use me against his brothers in who knows what way.

"Not you, though, darling," he says, and his tongue curls around the term of endearment. "Have you come to let me out to play?"

"Maybe I've come to return the favor you bestowed on me the other day," I say, running a finger down that glass again. He tracks the move, and I draw my gaze back up to his. "A knife to your throat?"

"Oh," he draws out the word, shaking his head. "I'd love to watch you play with blades."

Something dark shivers inside me, a temptation and craving I can't ignore.

"Lock," I whisper his name, wanting to tell him off, to snap at him, *something*—

"Mmm," he murmurs, the sound coming from deep in his chest. "Say that again."

I swallow against the urge to do whatever the hell he says. "Why did you risk capture?" I ask as a million questions storm through my mind.

"Who says I did?"

"They've been searching for you for a year," I say. "Your brothers and the All Plane guard."

"Both love to task themselves with impossible missions," he says coolly.

"You evaded them the entire time," I say, tilting my head. "Why risk taking me? Drawing their attention?"

A sly grin shapes his lips, something flickering in his eyes as he studies me. "Clever, darling," he says, then shrugs. "I let them take me."

"Let them?"

"Of course," he says. "If I didn't want to be found, I wouldn't be."

"Why?" I ask. "You're wanted across the realms. Your legend has reached the Shattered Isle. Why let them take you now?"

His grin deepens at my use of the word *legend*. "Maybe I heard about a certain bonding ceremony and felt it was within my right to take part."

My heart pounds against my chest. Even though he wasn't present at the ceremony, it doesn't change the fact that I'm bonded to *each* of the princes of the All Plane. Which means I belong to Lock as much as the rest.

I blow out a breath, trying to get a grip. His own brothers locked him up. And sure, after what he's accused of doing—and what he tried to do to me—even *I* feel safer with this glass between us, but he's not my blood.

"Maybe I grew tired of hiding," he adds when I don't respond.

"Tired of murdering innocent people in their sleep?" I clap back.

Lock freezes on the other side of that glass, and the hair on the back of my neck stands on end. "Rumors are rarely true," he says, his tone sharp.

"Usually rooted in truth," I fire.

He leans down, having to bend to meet me eye to eye because he's so damn tall. "People believe what they want to believe," he says, and I flinch at the hurt in his gaze. "How easy it is to call me a monster when there is a pane of glass between us."

I tip my chin. "Forgive me if I don't weep for you," I say, narrowing my gaze as I trail my fingers along my neck. His eyes track the move. "You seemed content to slice my throat the other day. Are you saying you're not the villain people say you are? Your own brothers have you locked away—"

"I never said they were the smartest brothers," he cuts me off. "And if you want to cast me as the villain? Fine. You would never try to get to know me, anyway." There is a hint of sadness in his words that I'm certain he doesn't mean to let slip, and it tugs on that connection I feel sizzling between us.

I sigh, studying him, parting my lips to say something, anything, but he beats me to it.

"They were never going to let me meet you," he says, rising to his full height and striding to a lounge chair facing the glass. He drops into it, and I'm once again taken aback by how tall he is, his muscled limbs dominating the large chair.

"I'm here now," I say, and he smirks.

"By your own foolishness," he says, but light dances in those eyes that look more green than blue now.

I shrug. "Maybe I'm not afraid of you."

"Liar," he says, then tilts his head. "Are you here to kill us all?"

I flinch at his blunt question, floundering in my own mind for a moment before recovering. "I'm your wife," I say, grinding out the words. "Your brothers' wife."

His eyes rake over my body, and every place he looks flares to life. He's accused of slaughtering hundreds of people across the realms. He entered my mind without my permission. How can I be hit with such want and need with that look?

It's the bond. That's all it adds up to.

I try to make myself believe the words. But maybe they're lies. Maybe I'm just as much a villain as him.

"Talon thinks you're here to destroy us all," he says casually, as if he's discussing the weather.

I keep my spine straight. "I'm here to mend the wounds between our realms."

"Letting me out of here would be a good start at healing," he says, and my eyes flicker to the control panel before snapping back to him.

"To do what?" I ask, breathless. "Slaughter me? Your brothers?"

A breath and he's against the glass again. I jump, but I don't dare step away. I hold that fiery gaze despite the fear clinging to my veins.

"Only one way to find out, darling," he says, the tone of a lover, not a threat. He inhales deeply, as if he can drink in my scent through the glass. Maybe he can, because his eyes darken. "Tor has claimed you," he says, almost laughing. "Was he gentle, darling? Did my warrior brother take it easy on you?"

I swallow hard, and words tangle in my throat.

He shakes his head, his hair shifting on his shoulders, and I hate how much I want to touch the strands to see if they feel like silk. "Was it enough to make you shake? Make you moan? Because from the look of you, you need a bit more danger to make you truly come undone."

Ice kisses my palms at the way he's laying me bare, as if he knows how my body sang when Tor's lightning crackled against my skin, the mixture of pleasure and pain bringing me to life in a way I never knew existed. Frost spiderwebs its way over the glass where my hands touch, and his eyes light up at the sight.

"Oh, yes, darling," he says as he steps back to admire my power. "I daresay I'm right."

I reel in my power, shushing the climbing panic and terror. Not from him, because for some unhinged reason, I'm not scared of him. It's of myself, of the way I'm responding to him, to the way I'm dying to break the glass with my ice and let him loose.

"Cari!" Steel's voice rings out as he rounds the corner, Tor not two steps behind him.

I draw back from the glass, folding my arms behind my back but not dipping my head.

Steel's arms wind around me as if he can shield me from his brother's words or his power. I'm not sure which. "What are you doing down here?"

Tor looks down at me, a brow cocked before he glances at Lock, who seems perfectly content behind that glass.

"I was exploring the ship," I explain.

"No one gave you permission to do that," Talon snaps as he comes around the corner. I tense at his words, and Steel's grip around me tightens.

"She doesn't need permission," Steel snaps, then he shifts to look down at me. "But I wish you would've told me. I could've—"

"I didn't need an escort," I say, then glance at Tor, then Talon. "Were any of you going to tell me you locked my fourth husband in a damn cage down here?"

Steel's mouth drops, and Tor eyes me like he'll scold me for my tone, but I don't care right now. I'm bonded to Tor, will soon be bonded to Steel, too, no doubt. And even if I never complete it with Talon or Lock, I still…

I still feel like I'm theirs, and they're mine.

At least, for now.

"It's hardly a cage," Talon groans, and I roll my eyes, pointing to the control panel.

"Trapped is trapped," I argue. "No matter how pretty the room is."

Lock grins at me, then cocks a brow at Talon as if to say *she gets it.*

And that alone has me trembling.

Because what am I furious about? Lock tried to kidnap me in the Air Realm. Why am I defending him? And how can I be mad at the princes for locking him up when my own father sent me here to kill them? *Or* am I angry simply because of that damn bond calling me to Lock, screaming at me that caging him is wrong?

"You understand the difficulty of this situation," Steel says. "We're all still trying to figure out the best thing to do," he admits, and I soften in his embrace, at the sound of his words. He means it. I can feel that as easily as I can feel Tor's irritation as he glares at Lock through the glass.

Lock shrugs as if they're holding some silent conversation.

I step out of Steel's embrace, needing space to calm my nerves. I'm about to apologize to all of them when Talon snatches me up by the arm, slamming me against the glass.

Tor's lightning buzzes on his hands as he holds Steel back.

Lock is behind me, staring down at me with a murderous look.

One that isn't as fierce as Talon's as he holds me there. He smells like leather and whiskey, and I hate that I shift against the press of his body on mine. He's unaffected, glaring down at me like he's contemplating slicing my throat right here. Ice storms through my body, chilling my skin, but he doesn't flinch. In fact, his eyes shudder, almost as if he welcomes the sting of the brutal cold.

"If you ever wander where you're not wanted again," Talon grinds out the words, glancing at Lock before focusing on me again. "I'll throw you in there with him. See if you survive *that*." He hits the glass so hard I flinch as he shoves off the wall, storming out of sight.

I hate that I stand there, trembling from the power he radiated, from the anger I can feel rising in Tor, from the concern I see on Steel's face, and from the heat calling behind me from Lock.

I push off the glass, shaking off the anger, the terror, the worry, and straighten my spine. "So," I say, happy my voice is holding strong when the very foundations of my soul feel like they're crumbling. Because I'm starting to have a hard time telling the difference between my own heart's desires and the damn bonds pulsing to life inside of me. "What are we doing today?" I ask, linking one arm through Steel's, then Tor's.

Tor lets out a bellowing laugh, patting my arm in his as the brothers guide me away from Lock's cage. "Well played, little wife," Tor says. "Well played."

"We're just about to dock in Corteran City," Steel explains. "It's within the Fire Realm. We thought you'd like to see it."

"You thought right," I say, letting them lead me through the ship, far away from Lock.

But even as we step out of the ship and into the heart of a bustling village, I can't stop the bond from screaming, begging me to go back.

9

CARI

"*D*idn't you say the Corters are the ones who attacked the Air Realm?" I ask as Steel and Tor weave through the collection of intricately designed huts that pepper Corteran City.

There are larger wooden structures, but nothing as advanced as the Air Realm. Their land is undeniably expansive and beautiful, drenched in the orange glow of the setting sun. Mountains hug the base of their village, and a turquoise stream winds next to it. Beautiful, stunning, and once again, new to me.

I silently—and for the first time—question why I was never allowed to see these realms. Perhaps my father could use the excuse of worrying over my safety as his only living heir, but something nags me with the thought. Especially since the princes have no problem taking me into the heart of the Corteran market now—even with the known tense lines that lie between my isle and these people.

Even Talon stalks behind us, his icy stare firmly on anything but me, regardless of how many times I look back at him. Not that I want to make amends. I'm simply checking to see if he has a knife aimed at my back.

"Indeed," Tor answers, a deep groove between his eyebrows.

"Then why are we here?" I whisper, my powers on high alert. The Corters seem harmless enough, carrying on about their business, carting things to their huts or offering wares at their market booths, but their thirst for power is unquestionable. If the princes stopped them from taking over the Air Realm territory, shouldn't we be avoiding them now?

"We come here once a year to remind them of the reasons they shouldn't attack innocent cities," Tor says.

"We have a tentative peace with them, and our visits help maintain that," Steel adds.

I nod, understanding flickering through me, but it does nothing to ease the powers poised at my fingertips. This place is not nearly as welcoming as the Air Realm, but I can see hope in a majority of the people's eyes. Even gratitude in some. I loose a breath, doing my best to smile at the onlookers as we buy more things we don't need, just so we can support their economy. This aspect of the princes I adore.

Some Corters go so far as to bow and offer verbal thanks to my husbands, and I find myself relaxing the more welcoming the people become. By the time we decide to have dinner at one of their taverns, I've almost forgotten that these people were once at war with mine.

Wait, not mine.

Theirs.

Shit. When did I start thinking of their wars as mine?

I suck in a sharp breath, desperate to clear my mind.

Steel orders for me after Talon and Tor place theirs, and we relax at a warm wooden table. Tor is on my right, Steel on my left, and Talon, of course, sits on the other side of the table, not bothering to look at me.

I try to ignore the bite of his earlier words, the threat he issued. Would he really throw me to Lock's mercy if I "misbehaved" again? Or is he just waiting for an excuse to lock me up too? Will he ever see me as anything other than a Shattered Isler?

Will you ever see them as anything other than the villains?

Yes, I already do. Which is as dangerous as it is reckless. But I can't deny it. Can't deny that bond simmering between all of us. Especially Tor's, now that we've bonded. And just the thought has me wanting more. Wanting to lose myself in him or Steel for who knows how long. An escape as much as a fantasy, one where I don't have to be the villain in their story, and they don't have to be the ones in mine.

Dinner passes in a blur of jokes from Tor, history from Steel, and silence from Talon. The meal is so delicious, I barely even notice the brother that won't bother to look at me. And it's almost comical, since it seems everyone else in the tavern can't *stop* looking at me.

I wish I can say it's because of the form-fitting clothes I wear, or the slight dusting of kohl I slipped over my eyes before venturing out here. I wish even more that I can say it's because of my beyond god-like husbands, but it's not any of those things. As evening descends into night, the tavern has filled with more and more Corters, these groupings looking more like mercenaries back from a hunt and less like the peaceful citizens we'd seen at the market. And more than half of them are inebriated.

The strong mead and sparkling wine overflows at this place, and it's clearly one of their specialties as more patrons order and guzzle the drinks down. And I'm all for indulging. I've already had a glass and a half of the sparkling wine, and Tor is on his fourth mug of mead. Talon and Steel remain stone sober at our sides, but only Talon looks sullen.

Still, I can't stop the twisting in my stomach as more and more eyes are cast my way. Talon can't see because his back is turned, and Tor is too busy recanting a warrior's tale to a small group that has clustered around our table. Steel is laughing quietly at his story and not paying one ounce of attention to the party across the room. The ones who can't stop giving me death glares.

I steady my breathing as the server clears our plates, and I decline a refill when she offers one for my glass. My instincts are roaring, ice kissing my palms every time one of the Corters' eyes catches mine. They're a fascinating realm and people, their bodies built like boulders and horns winding from the top of their heads, and I can't help but calculate just how quickly they can kill someone with them.

Steel's laughter deepens, joining Tor's, and the sound skitters along my bones in the most delightful way. There is a warmth and longing there I can't deny, and I'm honestly just too tired to keep doing so. I try to tell myself to relax, to give in to their ease around these people, but my instincts have never guided me wrong before, and every hair is standing at attention on my neck.

The group behind Talon is clearly in the midst of a heated argument, and every so often, a head or hand jerks my way, followed by a succession of growls and slurs.

But, to be fair, they've probably never seen someone from the Shattered Isle. Maybe that's all it is. They don't want me infringing on their territory anymore, and I really can't blame them. Peace between us and the other realms has always been tenuous, thanks to my new husbands' realm... or so I'd always been led to believe.

I'm just about to reach for Steel's hand to see if I can convince him to leave when I pause, my eyes tracking everything behind Talon in slow motion.

First, I see each of the five Corters in the angry group shove away from their table.

Second, I watch as they stomp toward us, looks of disgust curling their lips.

Third, I make a realization with horrible clarity.

It's not *me* they've been sneering at with hate in their eyes.

It's *Talon*.

My heart thuds against my chest, and in one blink, everything speeds up again.

The leader of the group draws a gleaming dagger from his sleeve, drawing it upward, eyes focused on the back of Talon's neck.

I leap from my seat, so fast and frantic that Steel jolts back, Tor at his side. The loud tavern has offered the would-be killers cover, and my husbands haven't noticed their intent.

But it doesn't matter.

Not when I land atop the table, dead center in front of Talon, a long sword of ice forming in my right hand. Talon's eyes go lethal as he looks up at me, reaching for something inside his blazer pocket—

I thrust my sword behind his head, the clang of the Corter's dagger ringing loudly as it halts against my weapon of ice.

Talon blinks twice, whirling around to face the Corter who wears an equal look of shock on his face.

"Run," I say, baring my teeth just a little as I look down at the angry group. "And I'll spare your lives."

The leader growls, drawing his dagger back and lunging for Talon again.

I jump, dropping in front of Talon as I shift into a defensive position. "Don't say I didn't warn you," I say, and block his attempt to sink his blade between my breasts.

It takes Tor and Steel only seconds to catch on to what's happening, and they flank my left and right in a blink, Talon still behind me.

The entire group registers the threat, and screams erupt as each one advances toward us. My sword crashes against blade after blade as I defend each hit aimed for me or one of my husbands. Regardless of Talon's disdain for me, he doesn't deserve to be stabbed in the back.

"Have you no honor?" I snap, sending the leader soaring backward several feet. Tor has rendered two of the Corters into useless puddles on the floor, his lightning making the air taste like white fire.

Steel's hand clenches tight around one's throat as he hauls him overhead, a snapping sound echoing throughout the room before he tosses him toward the table they once occupied.

"He killed my brother! He owes us blood!" the leader growls at me, and I spare a glance at Talon, who is battling the last remaining Corter.

Talon pushes two black button-looking pieces that sit atop the backs of his hands, and I watch, near gaping, as armor spiderwebs outward from the contraption, covering his body. In seconds, he's transformed into something otherworldly, something even more lethal and beautiful than his palace in the sky. One hit, that's all it takes to split the Corter's skull. His armor is *that* powerful.

A sharp slice of heat glides across my raised forearm, trailing in a slope over my chest. I grind my teeth, snapping my attention back to the leader, who I obviously shouldn't have taken my eyes off of. Not even for the second it took me to assess Talon.

His dagger is stained with my blood, and my powers surge in a fury. Tor lets out a warrior's roar, as if he can feel the wound himself through the bond. But he's not fast enough. Spears of ice storm from my body, shooting out in needle-sharp points, sinking into the Corter's gut and shoulders and knees, until he's pinned to the wall behind him.

The dagger he cut me with clatters to the floor, and he doesn't have time enough to scream before I send a final spear of ice through his throat.

The tavern is silent save for our heaving breaths, the rest of the patrons smartly fleeing the second the fight broke out. A clinking and whirring sounds, and I spin around to see Talon's armor retreating back into those smooth black buttons on his hands. His expression is equal parts anger and confusion, but he's blurring around the edges.

"I warned them." I breathe the words, wondering if he's angry that I killed the creature instead of incapacitating him. It's not in my nature to kill ruthlessly—I've only had to do it a few times at home when visiting the Dark Realm at our isle's edge—but once blood is drawn? All bets are off. Maybe the All Plane realm operates under different rules, but if *any* of the stories I've heard are accurate, that isn't true.

"Wife," Steel says, his voice full of concern. I spin to face him, my brow furrowing at how my vision seems dulled, a ghost trailing everything as I lock eyes on him.

"You're hurt?" Worry coats my tone as I try to lift my arm to point at the blood splattered across his chest, but my muscles are suddenly so damn heavy.

He shakes his head, and the floor tilts beneath my feet. Steel catches me before I hit the ground, cradling me against his chest. "Fucking Corters," he spits. "The dagger was laced with poison."

"A dagger meant for you, brother," Tor growls at Talon.

"We need to get her back to the ship," Steel says.

There is some hesitation, and I wonder for the briefest of moments if they're having a silent conversation about letting me die. They certainly couldn't be blamed for it, and the peace between our realms will still hold by honor. They'd just have the bonus of not being shackled to me.

"Fast," Talon demands. "I have an antidote."

Their voices mix in my mind, my eyes suddenly heavy.

"Cari," Steel says, the word a demand on his tongue.

I try to look at him, but a blanket of darkness falls over me, too heavy to fight off.

10
STEEL

I sit at Cari's bedside, elbows on my knees, my chin resting on my raised fists, as I wait for her to stir. Talon had only stayed long enough to give her the antidote, and Tor had gone to check on Lock an hour ago.

I pass the time by envisioning the deaths of the Corters over and over again. Had I known they would injure and poison my new wife, I would've made them suffer. Drawn out the kill.

Fury storms through my blood.

We've been traveling for a few hours. She should rouse any minute now. Talon, despite his open dislike of our new wife, administered the antidote the second we made it on the ship, and it's been working to rid her blood of the poison since.

She saved his life.

I swallow hard. She could've let that Corter sink his blade into Talon's neck—Tor and I wouldn't have blinked twice at her inability to save him. She could've used the opportunity to rid herself of his disgust, just as he could've done the same with her.

But neither one of them allowed the other to die. It fills my chest with what is likely an impossible hope for the future, and it *almost* dulls the rage pulsing in my gut.

Almost.

Cari stretches in the bed, her legs and arms straightening, but her eyes remain closed. I drop to my knees beside the bed, smoothing my hand over hers as she fights off the deep sleep.

Fuck, she's gorgeous.

And deadly.

Watching her tonight, the way she wielded that power inside her, shaping that beautiful ice into weapons hungry for blood, made her feel more like *ours* than ever before. She defended Talon in the same way I knew she'd defend me or Tor. Talon can spout his bullshit all he wants, but how can he possibly deny her now? Deny that she's one of us—an unexpected, delightful force to be reckoned with.

"Steel," Cari whispers, her brow furrowing as if she's struggling to get her eyes open.

My heart takes off at the sound of my name on her lips, as if she can already tell the difference between whose hand touches her own.

Pride swells in my chest with the thought, and I gently squeeze her hand. "I'm here," I say.

After a few attempts, she finally gets her eyes open. A few more breaths, and they clear of the fogginess I'm sure the poison and the antidote left her with.

She grins up at me as I move to sit next to her on the bed. "You're okay," she says. "You're not hurt?"

I shake my head, smoothing some of the hair away from her face. "It wasn't my blood," I say.

She nods, sighing. "And Tor? Talon? I can't remember…" She tilts her head, moving to sit up.

"They're fine. The dagger that cut you was poisoned," I say, grinding my teeth. "Talon healed you."

She raises her eyebrows at that, and the shock on her face makes me so damn sad, but I almost want to laugh at the same time.

"That's… uncharacteristically nice of him," she says, and then I *do* laugh. This female is more than I could've ever imagined. Always surprising me, always keeping me on my toes. "Did I cause a problem for you?"

I furrow my brow. "You saved my brother's life," I say. "How could that ever be a problem?"

"I slaughtered that Corter," she says, not a hint of regret in her eyes. "I know rash actions can sometimes be harmful to political situations and you and your realm have finally held peace with them—"

"Our realm," I correct her, then shake my head. "And no, Cari. You did what any one of us would've done under an attack like that." I grin at her. "You just did it a little more brilliantly than any of us." I slide my finger over her hand, noticing for the first time the skin of her palm is a few degrees cooler. "Your ice," I say. "Is amazing. Stronger than I would've ever guessed." I felt her power during the bonding ceremony, but I didn't have a clue how deep it ran.

"Does it scare you?" she asks almost timidly, as if others in her life had feared her instead of praising her for the warrior she is.

"Never," I say, my jaw clenching. "But when I realized you were poisoned? That scared me." I blow out a breath. "How do you feel?"

Cari takes a moment, her eyes trailing to the side as if she's doing a mental inventory. "I feel great," she says, then bites her lip.

"You don't need to be strong on my account," I assure her. "You know there is never any judgment from me."

She laughs. "That's not it," she says. "I don't feel any pain." She shrugs. "It's just that I feel…" I raise my brows at her. "Dirty."

I nod. "Getting the antidote to you was more important than washing the blood and grime off of your body," I explain, and thank the sun for it. Talon's antidote is so powerful it completely sealed the wounds on her arm and chest. "And then after… I didn't want to do that without your permission." Her eyes meet mine, a stunning mixture of shock and compassion, and I smile down at her as I push off the bed. "I'll run you a bath," I say, then hurry into her bathing chamber. I fill the tub with steaming water and a hefty amount of soothing milk balm that turns the water into a frothy shade of purple.

When I come back for her, she's moved off the bed, standing near the edge as she runs her hands over her body. I recognize the move of a trained warrior running a sweep for injuries. Who knew she'd be so well-trained, so powerful? Her father made no mention of it, and the fact that he didn't use her skills as a bargaining chip when vying for our alliance bothers me more than it probably should.

Who cares if she's as deadly as Talon feared?

She's ours.

"Can you manage on your own?" I ask, and she tilts her head. "Or would you like me to help you into the tub?"

She presses her lips together, something churning in her eyes. Heat slams into me, my blood pounding with *need*. The need to see her cared for, to claim her in every way possible. To complete our bonding process.

"Stay with me?" she asks, and I hate the uncertainty in her voice. As if she doubts herself, her position with me. As if I would ever leave her if she wants me here.

I suppose I'll have to fuck that right out of her.

"Come," I say, reaching out for her. Her eyes snap to mine as she gives me her hand. "Let's get you clean, wife."

Her breath catches as I lead her into the bathing chamber, the room filled with floral-scented steam. The lights are dimmed, but I can still see her pulse race as I gently turn her to face me.

Slowly, I reach for the end of her silk shirt, eying her as I start to tug it upward. She nods, raising her arms for me. I slide the fabric off her body, tossing it behind me. I swallow hard, my cock straining at the sight of her glorious breasts, her nipples peaked. She lowers her arms, reaching for the band of her pants, but I catch her wrists, stopping her.

I sink to my knees as I pull the pants down her long legs, marveling at every delicious inch of her. She's all sweeping curves and smooth skin, and she easily steps out of the pants as I throw them to join her shirt. The sight of her completely bare for me has a low growl rumbling in my chest.

"You're exquisite," I say, my voice ragged. All I want to do is part those beautiful thighs and taste her, but my wife expressed a need to me, and I will not let my own selfish desires impede that.

I stand, ridding myself of my clothes before I gather her into my arms. She gasps a little as I step into the deep tub, more than large enough for the both of us. I sink us into the hot water and relish the sigh she makes at the contact.

She doesn't immediately pull away when I release her. Doesn't rush to the other side of the tub. She stays right where she is, perched atop my lap, but cranes her head back far enough to soak her hair in the water.

"Are the tubs this big at the palace?" she asks, her eyes closing as she extends her arms through the water.

"Bigger," I say, smoothing my hands over her stomach and upward, daring to tease those peaked nipples.

She sits up straight, her hair falling in a silky wet curtain around her. "Bigger?"

I grin at her. "Much. Bigger."

Her smile is wide as she reaches behind me, the motion drawing her chest flush against mine. All I need to do is push her thighs apart, hook one leg on either side of my hips, and I can sink into her. My cock strains with the thought of it, with the need coursing through my blood.

She draws back slightly, bringing the bar of pine-scented soap that sat behind me. "Well, I can't wait for that," she says, lathering soap between her fingers. She shifts back a bit, her eyes churning with heat as she stands, raising her top half out of the water.

I stretch my arms on the marble behind me, content to watch her.

A smirk shapes her lips as she glides that soap over her neck, her arms, then her breasts. She takes her time there, her fingers experts as she teases herself and tortures me. I clench my jaw, telling my cock to calm the fuck down. I'm a grown male, for sun's sake. I can control myself while she—

Her hands move lower, her mischievous grin deepening as her hand dips under the water.

"Do you like what you see, Steel?" she asks, and I groan at the sound of my name on her tongue.

"I said you were exquisite," I say, letting my gaze trail over the length of her body, not missing a move she makes against herself. "Do you?" I ask, glancing down at myself. I already know her answer, had seen it in her eyes the first day she arrived. She hadn't been happy about just how attracted she was to each of us, but now?

Now she looks at me with unrestrained need in her eyes, and I soak up every drop.

"It should be a crime," she says, sinking into the water until it reaches her shoulders. She sets the soap back in its place behind me, bringing her body so damn close to mine again.

"What?" I ask, my heart pounding. I need this female more than I've ever needed anything in my life. That unsolidified bond inside me roars, begging me to haul her against me and pump into her until she screams. But right alongside the power of the bond is a pulse of lust, pure and raw and totally unrelated to our connection.

It's her.

Just her.

"How attractive you are," she answers, and grips my shoulders. The contact sears my skin, and I hiss as she laughs. She's brought ice to her fingers, the contrast with the steaming hot water a jarring surprise. She tilts her head as she lets the ice go, her grip loosening where she clings to me.

"What is it, wife?" I ask.

"Do you... not want to touch me?" she asks, doubt flickering over her features.

I growl, my hand darting up to grip her chin when she tries to look away from me. "That's *all* I want to do."

She holds my gaze, but I see the questions swimming there. And I hate it. Hate whatever is holding her back. Whatever is keeping her from believing my intentions with her.

I shift my other hand to her hip, yanking her closer to settle over my lap. The hot water sloshes around us, our bodies gliding against each other. "Feel that?" I ask, pressing my cock against her.

She gasps.

"You do that to me," I say, nipping at her bottom lip. "Since you walked onto this ship, I've wanted to sink into you. Wanted to claim you. Wanted to worship your body until there is no patch of skin I haven't tasted." She whimpers a bit at that, and I flick my tongue over her lips. "I told you from the beginning, I'll never take what isn't mine." She visibly swallows. "But if you keep giving me that look, the one where you're doubting yourself, I'm going to bend you over this bathtub and fuck you until you understand just how damn amazing you are."

She shudders above me, and I arch a brow at her. I've laid myself bare. Now it's her turn.

Her tongue darts out to wet her lips, her eyes jumping from mine to my mouth as she inches closer. It takes every ounce of strength I have not to move, to hold this game between us, to stretch out this anticipation so much it burns.

She lingers a breath before my lips, something hot and needy flashing in her eyes before she crushes her mouth on mine. I growl, my grip on her hip tightening, my other hand sliding around to the back of her neck. I hold her there, willing my hips to remain still, to wait until she says what I need to hear.

"Fuck," I groan between her lips, her tongue gliding into my mouth. She rocks against my hard length, the warmth of the water making her slick against me. "Cari," I breathe, and she pulls back.

"I'm yours," she whispers the words, and it's all I need to capture her mouth again. This time, I sink my hand between us, sliding my fingers over her sensitive flesh. She gasps, rocking into my touch.

"Say it again," I demand, teasing her warmth. I glide my fingers over her clit with light touches. She chases my hand, silently begging for more. "Say it."

"I'm. Yours." She forces out the words between breaths, and I claim her mouth as I sink one finger inside her, then two. Fuck, she's nothing but pure searing silk as I pump her. I kiss her hard, using my tongue to show her exactly what I'm going to do to her in a minute. For now, I'm enjoying this too damn much.

"Steel," she sighs against my mouth, rocking against my fingers as she chases her pleasure. And damn, it's delicious to watch. Her nails dig into my shoulders as I use the heel of my palm to grind against her clit, giving her just enough pressure to drive her mad with need.

I slip my free hand around her waist, resting on the small of her back as I push her harder into my other hand, keeping her there as she rocks atop me. She throws her head back, tossing her wet hair over her shoulder as she moans.

"Steel, yes," she says, arching her head back, the angle putting her right where she needs me against my fingers.

"Fucking beautiful," I say, loving watching her slowly break apart. This wild, strong, amazing female is at the mercy of my hands, and she doesn't care. She's mine, and she fucking knows it.

I curl my fingers inside her, teasing them against that spot deep inside her—

"Steel!" She clenches around my fingers, her lips parting on the sweetest moan as she flutters around me. I continue to stroke and pump her through the throes of her orgasm, my cock rock hard and pulsing at the sight.

She goes limp as I gently slide my fingers out of her and kiss her again. Her hands dip beneath the water, reaching for me, but I quickly grip her hips and spin her, hefting her sweet ass onto the side of the tub.

"I'm not even remotely close to done with you yet," I growl, pushing her knees apart. I groan at the sight of her swollen, glistening flesh and don't waste a second before dipping my head between her thighs.

She gasps, her fingers tangling in my hair as I run my tongue from her entrance to clit and back again in teasing strokes. Her grip tightens, and I grin before plunging my tongue inside her, her flavor bursting on my tongue. "Fuck," I groan. "You taste like heaven." And she does. Like salted caramel. I'm instantly addicted.

"Steel," she says, breathless. Her thighs are trembling, and the intensity of my feasting has her drawing back. I dart my arm out, wrapping it around her ass and holding her right where she is. "I…" She gasps as I plunge and lap and suck. "I'm…"

She loses track of her words as I continue to devour her, relishing the taste of her pussy on my tongue. I grip one thigh with my free hand, pushing it out further so I can go deeper. She clenches, her muscles tightening as she rides up to that edge again. I flatten my tongue over her clit, giving her the shove she needs.

An incoherent moan rips from her lips, and I lick her as she comes apart in my mouth. Only when her body relaxes again do I pull away, and it's damn reluctantly at that. I draw back, smiling down at her as I lick my lips. "I could do that for hours," I say, and a whimper escapes the back of her throat.

And I really fucking could, but right now? I really want to know how that delicious pussy feels around my cock.

I step up the stairs in the tub, climbing out and onto the soft fur rug on the heated tile floor. Cari spins on the edge of the tub, her lips parting at the sight of me, her eyes widening at my hard cock.

I grin at her. "You think you're ready to take me?" I ask, eying her. "Or do you need a few more orgasms before you can?"

She trembles, and I patiently wait for an answer. I'm not small by any means, and I want this to be as painless as possible. But even when she gets used to taking me, I'll still make sure she comes multiple times before my cock ever gets near her. That's just how I operate.

"Where do you want me?" she asks, and *fuck me*, I nearly come from that submission alone. Somehow, I hold it together and scoop her off the edge of the tub. I don't go far, setting her down in front of the marble countertop. I face her toward the giant mirror, ensuring she can see herself *and* me towering over her from behind.

"Here," I say, and then gently nudge her ankles apart with my foot as I press against her spine with my hand. She instantly bends over the counter, her breath catching from the cool marble against her heated skin. I laugh softly. "Payback for the ice," I tease, and she laughs too.

I take my time eying her in this position, my fingers trailing over the line of her spine and lower, before going back up to her neck. She arches and trembles under my touch, a string of need ready to snap despite everything I've just given her. Her appetite for me only makes me harder, and I stop playing.

I wind her long hair around my right hand, tightening and tugging until her chins tips up. "Eyes up," I demand, and she obeys. They're as heated as mine when she looks at me—looks at *us*—in the mirror.

My blood races as I close the inch of space between us, situating my cock at her entrance. I hiss as the heat of her teases my head. She sighs and her hands splay against the marble.

With one smooth, hard stroke, I plunge into her. Fuck, her heat hugs my cock, the fit perfect. She moans, and I give her a few seconds to adjust to my size. But she's slick from before, and she pushes her ass backward, urging me to move.

So I do.

I smooth my free hand down her spine, then curl it around her hip, leaving my other tangled in her hair. I grip that hip and pull all the way out of her before slamming home again in one deep stroke.

"Yes," she says, her head still arched back from my hold on her hair.

I grin at her in the mirror, then sink into her again, relishing the way her eyes close briefly with each thrust before opening again. She pushes back as I pull out, not letting me leave her for long.

"Fuck," I growl, gripping her harder as I thrust into her again and again.

"You feel amazing," she says, her words breathless as she takes me to the hilt over and over.

I watch her in the mirror, devouring every pleasure-filled look, every lust-maddening gaze of her eyes as I drive her toward that edge again.

The power in me grows so sharp I can taste it, and hers rises just as fiercely. The bond between us practically glows with it, her ice curling lovingly around my impossible, unflinching strength. They weave together, braiding into something new and endlessly powerful, until I can taste her ice on my tongue.

"Harder," she demands, and I yank on her hair, arching her head back until her neck is fully exposed. I want to run my tongue and teeth over that neck, but that will have to come later.

"I don't want to hurt you," I say, stilling inside her. "My power—" My words die as she pushes back against me.

"I can feel your power," she says. "You won't hurt me, Steel."

My muscles strain against the need to pound into her, to drop the restraints I've always held on myself during sex. Absolute control has always been necessary when I can accidentally kill someone if I'm not careful.

"I can take it," she insists, her tone drenched in need as she rocks back into me again. Harder this time.

"Fuck, Cari," I groan. "Are you sure?"

"I want all of you," she says. "Don't hold back."

Those words snap the leash I always hold on myself and I drive into her in a way I've never done with anyone before. She takes me, urging me on with her moans, her ragged breaths.

"Yes," she moans, smacking a palm against the marble as I up my pace.

"Fucking hell," I growl as I submit fully to the need between us, both our bodies' and the bond's demands. Harder, faster. I drive into her until she's clenching around my cock in the most delicious way.

"*Steel.*" My name is a plea on her lips as she flutters around my cock, her orgasm drawing out my own as release barrels down my spine. My vision goes black as I empty into her, and I growl from the pleasure in it.

Seconds later, I fold myself over her back, releasing her hair as I plant gentle kisses up and down her spine. We catch our breath, and I come back to reality, panic clutching my heart.

"Did I hurt you, wife?" I ask, gently sliding out of her and turning her to face me.

She looks up at me with hooded eyes as mine race over her body. I curse myself at the red marks on her hip where I gripped her. I drop to my knees, kissing the offended skin before looking up at her.

"I'm sorry," I say. Having unlimited strength is a gift, but when I lose hold of my control like I just did? It can be dangerous. And yes, she's strong, but the last thing I ever want to do is hurt her.

"Are you kidding me?" she asks, reaching for my chin and tipping it so I have to look up at her.

I arch my brows at her, and she laughs, shaking her head. "Steel," she sighs. "You're…" Something makes her breath catch, and she blinks away moisture in her eyes as she smiles down at me. "You're perfect," she finally says, and I rise to stand before her. "And I'm stronger than I look."

I smooth my hand over her hair. "I know," I say.

Stars flicker in her eyes as she grins up at me. "Then let's see if you can *hurt* me some more," she teases, and I laugh as the bond between us flares bright and strong.

Complete.

Cari and I are now linked for as long as our hearts beat.

I inhale deeply, relishing the feel of that connection before sweeping an arm beneath her knees and holding her to my chest. I stride through the bathing chamber and gently lay her on the bed.

"Let's see how much you can handle, *wife*."

11

CARI

"You too now?" Talon's voice is pure disappointment, and I pause before rounding the corner to the dining hall.

"Yes, Talon," Steel says. "Me too."

Talon releases a heavy sigh, and I can just picture him pinching the bridge of his nose.

I swallow down the sting of his disapproval. After I saved him, and he gave me the antidote to the damn poison, I thought maybe we'd be able to come to some sort of…non-hate relationship. From the way he's speaking to Steel—no doubt about our newly completed bond—I assumed wrong.

"Brother," Tor chimes in, and my senses prickle with awareness. The bond between each of us reaches out, stretching and tugging. I take a step away from the room, not wanting either of them to feel our connection and catch me eavesdropping. "You can't fight the pull forever."

"Sure I can," Talon grumbles.

"She *saved* your life," Steel argues.

"Yeah, and to what end?" Talon asks.

"Maybe," Tor says, "so you wouldn't have to endure the pain of a blade in your neck?"

Talon huffs. "You two are blind to what she truly is."

"And what's that?" Steel asks.

"A traitor!" Talon snaps.

I flinch at the bitterness in his voice.

"You're wrong," Tor says, but his declaration does nothing to ease that knot in my chest.

"You two have to agree with me," Talon says. "Her father sent her here for a reason. And it sure as hell wasn't to bring peace between our realms. He's slaughtered thousands of innocent people for decades without apology. Every chance he gets, he's sent his night-shrouded armies into our lands and wiped out the most defenseless among us. He's the reason we've ordered the less populated villages to move within our royal territory."

Shock crystalizes like ice over my skin. Is that true? Did Father really do that? Every time he sent out the armies, he said it was to give aid to those affected by the carnage from the All Plane realm attacks.

"Right," Steel says, and the lack of shock in his voice nearly crushes me. "All of that is true. But none of that pertains to Cari."

"She doesn't know about any of that," Tor adds.

"You two can't be this stupid. Of course, she knows. She's his *only* heir. Do you honestly think he kept her in the dark this entire time?"

Silence eats up the space.

"Holy shit," Talon says. "You do."

"She *doesn't* know," Steel says with finality. "Every time I mention any of our history, there is nothing but shock and defiance in her eyes."

Talon groans. "Why would the king do that? Keep his own daughter in the dark to what he's capable of?"

"He obviously wanted her to think of us as enemies," Tor says. "He's probably been planning this proposal of marriage and bonding since her conception."

My stomach hits the floor.

"Exactly," Talon says. "Whether or not she knows about his true nature, he's raised her to hate us. You've heard from her own lips, she thinks we've dance in the blood of her people. And now she's bonded to the two of you. Do you think someone who has grown up thinking of us as monsters would so easily bond with you two without a purpose?"

The breath stalls in my lungs.

Silence.

I hate that I want Tor and Steel to keep defending me, to keep assuring Talon he's wrong. But I do. I want it so badly.

He *isn't* wrong, though. Not entirely. Father did send me here on a mission. Father did raise me with intent. It's only since meeting them, *being* with them, that I've questioned the reasons behind everything. And after what I've just heard?

How can I trust anything?

Even my heart is betraying me.

Tor and Steel, the bonds we share, the connections I can't deny, the way they make me feel alive, feel challenged, feel worthy, it's all shoving me toward a truth I can't ignore—

The scraping of a chair sounds, and I back up another step.

"She is our wife," Steel says. "Tor has completed the bonding process, and so have I. I can *feel* her, Talon. We can feel her intentions, her *heart*. She is good, and so much better than you give her credit for." He sighs. "One day soon, brother," he continues. "You'll have to contend with that."

"And one day soon, *brother*," Talon growls back. "You'll both have to come to terms with the fact that your new wife may be a viper biding its time in your beds."

Angry tears bite the backs of my eyes, and I spin on my heels, rushing down the long, winding corridors. My mind spirals, rage bubbling to the surface. Not at Talon, but at *me*.

I've walked a thin line since I boarded this palace in the sky, and it's time I pick a side. Do I believe them? Do I let their words and touches erase every story ever told to me about them? The ones where they're the monsters in the sun's light, sweeping over my people like a plague and showing no remorse afterward?

I breeze around corners and down more hallways, simmering without paying attention to where I'm going. I can't breathe around the battle raging in my heart, the one screaming at me to end this one way or another.

The mission.

The idea of killing them in their sleep had been so easy to think about before...

But now?

The pain goes deeper, like my very soul is lashing out against the notion.

I can't—

"Hello, darling," Lock's voice jolts me, and I blink out of my internal battle, only now realizing where I've gone.

Lock sits in an armless wing-backed chair, one long leg crossed over the other as he thumbs through a book. He doesn't bother looking up at me.

"Lost again?" he asks, eyes still on his book.

A prickle of awareness mixed with fear raises the hairs on the back of my neck. I can feel our bond reaching toward the glass cage, aching to be completed. I wonder if he feels it too? But I quickly dismiss the idea, especially since he doesn't even look up from the book. Perhaps monsters like him aren't capable of feeling anything beyond their own selfish desires. But me? I can feel it, and I wonder if that's how I ended up here during my fuming.

"I don't know," I admit.

He finally looks up, and night damn me, those eyes hit mine and my chest expands with *relief.* As if all I needed to ease my tension was to look at him, to hear his voice.

He shuts the book in one motion, then strides toward the glass. He towers over me, and I'm not entirely surprised by how close I stand his cage. I can't fight the draw of the bond, and he's perfectly contained now. But if he got out?

A shudder ripples down my spine. He'd likely tear me to pieces just to spite Tor and Steel before taking over the ship and wreaking havoc across the realms. Talon may very well assist him.

"Do you know anything, darling?" he asks, his voice a languid kind of relaxed. It's almost hypnotic, or would be if it he wasn't so insulting.

I glower up at him, somehow feeling so much smaller than normal in his presence. "I know a great deal of things," I fire back.

A slow, predatory grin shapes his lips. Lips I can't stop staring at. Night's *end*, what is wrong with me? It may be unclear and even unbelievable to me that Tor and Steel are monsters, but Lock? He most certainly is. He's held a knife to my throat. He's killed dozens of innocents in the past year alone. His brothers certainly haven't locked him up for no reason.

"You don't know the important things," he says, "if you keep crossing Talon's line of fire."

"Who says I'm doing that?"

"You wouldn't end up here for any other reason, would you? You're clearly on the hunt for information, and I assure you, going behind Talon's back will only result in your demise."

I straighten my shoulders at the threat. "I'm not looking for information."

He furrows his brow. "Why else would you be traipsing to my cage other than to trick me into giving up dirt on my brothers?"

I raise my brows at him. "Now there's an idea."

He laughs, but quickly stops, as if he didn't mean to let it slip. "Then why *are* you here, darling?"

I shiver at the way he says *darling*, hating that my body reacts to the endearment.

It's the bond. Just the bond.

I fold my arms over my chest. "I didn't mean to come here," I admit. "I heard them arguing and… wound up here."

His smile deepens. "Ah, do tell."

Heat flushes over my skin, his voice curling around my body like a caress. "Me," I say. "What else would they be arguing about?"

"There is an abundance of things," Lock says. "What they'll do with me, for one. If they'll hand me over to our father to let him publicly execute me or if they'll risk letting me free to spare my life."

I swallow hard, ice kissing my palms. "They're thinking about freeing you?" I ask.

He tilts his head. "Does that scare you?"

I shake my head.

"Liar," he coos, the deep tenor like a sweet lull to my senses. I stumble forward until I touch the glass.

I blink a few times, and he laughs, this one so different from before.

"You're much easier to get inside of than I thought," he says, and I look up at him in confusion. "Maybe it's the bond," he continues, trailing his fingers down his side of the glass, pausing over where the apex of my thighs would be if I were in there with him.

My heart skips, but I don't move away like I know I should. There is a pane of glass between us, but I swear I can feel the heat from where his hands touch.

"You know Talon doesn't bluff, right?" he asks, and I nearly jolt from the change in conversation.

"What?"

"You said you know *a great deal* of things," he says. "I'm wondering if you know well enough that if you keep provoking Talon, he'll make good on his promise. He'll throw you in here with me and never look back."

Ice skates down my spine, and his grin deepens.

"Do you know what I'll do to you, then?"

I swallow hard, my mouth suddenly dry. "No," I whisper.

"Do you want me to show you?" he asks.

Curiosity clambers inside me, begging and aching. "Yes."

His eyes light up, shock and respect filling them. "Close your eyes."

My instincts roar to keep them open, but I do as he says. Silence is almost a ringing thing in my ears as I wait, my heart thumping hard against my chest. He's behind the glass, safely locked away. What harm can he really do to me here? But I can't possibly cower in his presence; he'd pounce all over that like the predator he is.

I'm about to open my eyes, my patience growing thin at whatever game he's playing, but then I feel *something* at the edge of my mind. The bond inside me flares to life, practically purring at the unfamiliar presence nudging my mind, a kind of smoky warmth that strokes and begs.

I give, opening my mind to that presence, and then the darkness behind my closed lids vanishes. It's a familiar sensation, just like when he'd had me captive on the bridge in the Air Realm. Only this time, I'm not in a room of darkness.

I'm on the other side of Lock's glass cage, the scent of snow and stars swarming me. A gleaming silver dagger kisses my throat, Lock wielding it as he towers over me. My spine presses hard against the wall, but that blade doesn't break my skin. I tremble, noticing just how much bigger he is than me with him this close.

"If your bastard of a father sent you here to kill my brothers," he says, his voice low and rough and promising. "No one will be able to hear you scream as I shred you apart."

I wonder if he can feel my shame, my regret, the conflict brewing in my soul since he's fully immersed in my mind?

"What if I'm here to find the best avenue to peace between our realms?" I ask, so careful not to move too much because of the blade.

He studies me, those blue-green eyes scanning the lines of my face, the curve of my lips. "I want that to be true," he whispers, shifting so his thigh presses between mine.

Warmth spirals in my core. He holds me in place, pushing against my heat. Pair that with the look in his eyes—which isn't at all murderous—and I'd wager this is more his style. A game. Quid pro quo. Only the fearless are worth his time.

I reach out mentally, wrapping myself around everything that is him in my mind—his scent, the sensation of mischief curling and teasing along my bones. I hold on to that feeling and then picture taking the knife from him.

Lock jolts backward as the dagger disappears on a phantom wind.

"Get out of my head," he says, eyes not at all amused anymore.

"But you're in mine," I say, stalking across the room of my own free will. To my surprise, he retreats until his knees hit that armless chair, and he sinks into it. My body rushes with the power in that, and I lean over him. "It's only fair."

"How? How are you doing this?" he asks, genuine interest coloring his eyes.

I look down at him. I really don't have an answer. "Not used to the victims whose minds you possess taking control of their actions?" I ask.

A muscle in his jaw flexes. "I don't enchant just anyone's minds."

"You have a code?"

"Yes," he growls, looking unraveled.

I have no idea what's giving me the power to have my own free will while he's enchanting my mind, but I'm all for it if it shakes him up this much. "What is that code?"

He narrows his gaze up at me. "I only tell that to the people I trust."

"Are there many of those?"

He gives me one shake of his head, and for a moment, I swear I sense sadness and even loneliness radiating across our weak bond.

He growls, jumping up, and his hand clenches my throat.

The sensation of choking is there, but I can't feel his hand on my skin. Not even as he pushes me back against that wall, reclaiming his power over the enchantment. I struggle to breathe as he glares down at me.

"You're on dangerous ground, darling," he says, and the phantom grip on my neck loosens enough for air to flood my lungs. "Don't play games you're not equipped to win." He drops his hand but doesn't back away.

I draw breath, then tip my chin as I hold his gaze. "Maybe you've been playing with the wrong partner, if you're so used to not being challenged."

He cocks a brow at me, then flashes me a devastating smirk. He presses one finger to my forehead—

I fall back against the wall outside his glass cage, my knees buckling as I sink to the floor.

"Oh, yes," he says. "I forgot to mention my enchantment has that effect on the body."

I toss him a vulgar gesture, and he laughs again. This one is as surprising as the first, and he shakes his head. He spins around, his long coat flaring about him before he returns to his chair, reclaiming his book as if nothing at all happened.

But I'd held some sort of power within that enchantment, and from his reaction, I know it isn't normal.

And as I manage to rise to my feet, he seems just as shocked that I can stand on my own so soon. Even if he won't look up at me, I can see that much in his eyes. I smirk, drunk with the power of shocking someone like him, and turn my back on his cell.

"Don't be a stranger, darling," he calls out once I've made it to the end of the hallway.

I pause, glancing over my shoulder. His eyes are on the book, but I can see the hint of a smirk there. I continue walking before I give in to the draw he has on me and mentally applaud myself.

I've just found an interesting new way in with Lock, and who better to help me settle the internal debate raging within me than with the brother who has no stake in this game at all?

12

CARI

"Aren't you afraid Talon will find out about our little visits, darling?" Lock asks from where he sits on the floor, his long legs stretched out before him. He leans against the wall, his head tipped up, eyes on the ceiling as he absently tosses a small bronze ball in the air over and over again.

I shake my head, even though he's not looking at me. "I'm not afraid of *you*. What makes you think I'm afraid of Talon?"

Lock catches the ball, his gaze slowly finding mine. The look is equal parts scrutiny, intrigue, and sex. I don't even think he *means* to be sexy and terrifying at the same time. It's simply effortless for him.

I don't shy away from the look, not anymore. It's been a week of me sneaking to his level. A week of endless conversations about nothing and everything.

Well, everything except his most recent past. His childhood? He's told me countless tales about him and his brothers, only solidifying my case for their goodness. The brothers he paints are nothing like the ones my father painted for me.

But Lock's reason for being trapped in this pretty glass cage? He won't touch on that topic.

I want to unearth his story, want to know the truth behind the monster. The one who has made me laugh, made me gasp, and given me plenty of intel on his brothers—but only the good stuff. It's clear how much he loves them, despite them locking him up. It has to count for something, and creates a slightly complicated yet imperfectly beautiful puzzle.

There are a couple of pieces missing, but I don't dare acknowledge who the empty spaces belong to.

Lock returns to throwing the ball in the air, and I tuck my knees closer to my chest. The floor is cold, the chill seeping through my silk shorts. Once again, I wish to be on the other side of the glass, lounging in one of those comfortable chairs while Lock indulges my questions.

I don't know if it's the glass between us or the fact that he has absolutely no reason to lie to me, but I speak more freely with him than I do with Tor or Steel. I'm open with them, but they... they've bonded with me and I with them. There are different stakes attached to those terms. They will always seek to ease my pain or lessen it, just as I would for them now. Lock has no such motivation. In fact, with what I've learned of him over the past week, he's prone to brutal truths over anything sugar-coated.

"Tell me about The Great War," I say, and my stomach twists. I've avoided this question in each of our secret chats this week, instead sticking to easier topics like their childhood and other, less influential battles.

He catches the ball, shifting his position on the floor to face me in one fluid motion. "I was wondering when you were going to find the courage to ask me."

I wet my lips, my heart racing. "I didn't lose my courage, so there was no need to find it."

Lock cocks a brow at me, and warmth spirals down my spine. "Sure, darling. Whatever you say. I'm sure you've avoided this question in particular, simply because you can't stand the thought of bloodshed." He eyes me, and I don't dare flinch. "It can't at all be because you're afraid of the truth and the fact that you know I'll give it to you, regardless of how painful."

I swallow the knot in my throat, cursing myself for opening my mouth. He sees me, right down to the very roots of my being. And I know that's bad, know that opens a door for him to rip me out by them in the end, but I don't care. We're only drawing nearer to the end of our journey, and I'm more conflicted than ever before. Lock has the answers I need, and a heart icy enough to bare the truth to me.

"Your silence says more than your words," he says when I haven't responded, and I merely shrug at him.

"I want to know," I say. "About the war that ended in a separation of our two great realms. Mine being the secluded one," I add for good measure. "I grew up hearing one thing, but Tor and Steel obviously were told a very different story."

"And you think I have the answers?" he asks, tilting his head.

"I know you do."

"How?" he challenges, those eyes flicking up and down my body as if he's trying to peel me back layer by layer until I'm raw and vulnerable for him to consume.

I steel my nerves. "Because you've seen it," I say boldly, and he blanches for a second before smoothing that calm, confident mask over his features.

"Who says?"

I roll my eyes. "So many challenges today," I say. "You didn't make me work this hard for the tales of your solstice traditions."

"Details about roasted ducks and pine trees differ vastly from recounts of sand and blood."

"Still," I say, sighing. "I know you've seen it because you're... *you*."

He barely stifles a laugh. "Such a clever little wife we have," he says, laying his hand flat over his chest. "I am me. Me am I. I never would have known."

I bite my lip, trying like hell not to laugh, but I can't help it. Especially when he smirks at me like that. "I keep forgetting to bring things from my room down here," I say. "So I can throw them at you when you're being a smartass."

"Your arm would grow very tired," he says.

I laugh again, then blow out a breath. "Your power," I say, knowing he won't indulge me until I've answered him. "With it, you can see into people's minds. Wield them, shape them, make them see entirely different worlds."

"I'm very impressive like that," he says, and I roll my eyes at him again.

"There's not a chance you didn't peek into your father's mind," I say without missing a beat, and all humor drains from his face. "You saw The Great War through his eyes. If not by stealth, then by him forcing your hand." I wouldn't put it past the All Plane king to make Lock witness the great battle to instill his values and loyalty to him.

Lock visibly swallows, and I'm not sure if I've ever seen him more rattled. Not even when I held power over him when he enchanted *my* mind. An old wound seems to reopen in his eyes as they go distant. They're more green than blue today, and they grow colder the longer he sits there, staring at a spot on the floor between us.

Something angry and hurt flickers along that incomplete bond between us, and a lump forms in my throat.

"Lock," I whisper his name like an apology for causing this pain, old and new.

He blinks, his eyes snapping to mine as he fully returns to the present. He clears his throat, a sharp sort of rage coating his gaze.

I sigh, seeing the wall he's built between us. Gone is the humor, the banter, the stories where he let down his guard and just *was* for a few blissful moments. In its place is the monster I've heard about.

"I'm done entertaining you for today, darling," he says, standing and waving a hand as if that alone will dismiss me.

I do stand, but instead of walking away, I press my hand against the glass, right over his chest. "I thought nothing scared you," I say.

He glares down at me. "Nothing scares the thing that *creates* terror."

"Liar," I say, shaking my head. "Whatever nerve I struck?" I look up at him, studying his eyes. They're vast and endless, just like the sea I love so much back home. "It *terrifies* you."

His jaw clenches as he silently argues with me.

I drop my hand, shrugging. "That's the thing about fear, Lock," I say as I back away from his cage. "Sometimes it's stronger when you battle it alone."

His lips part as if he'll say something, but he thinks better of it and closes his mouth. I dip my head to him. "Until next time," I say, then spin around, hurrying back toward my room.

The chill follows me, and it's not until I'm under the covers in my bed that my breathing eases. Sleep evades me, my mind racing. Because Lock *was* terrified and angry at whatever memory I'd dug up. And if it's enough to make *him*—the epitome of evil—fearful?

Then the truth behind The Great War is worse than I ever imagined.

And my future… *our* future, hangs in the balance.

13
CARI

"What stop is this?" I ask as the ship docks.

Mountains fill the view of the windows, their peaks dusted with snow. The land at their base is lush and green, with hundreds of yellow trees scattered throughout. A city is tucked into the trees, the small homes and buildings looking like they've been carved right from the land itself.

"This is the outer reaches of the Earth Realm," Tor answers, smiling down at me.

We've grown closer this past week. Each morning, we eat a quick breakfast together before heading to the ship's elaborate training room. He loves challenging me, sparring with me, and we've run through every weapon on the ship. Sometimes I win, other times he does, but it always ends with a shower and sex after.

"The last stop before we reach the All Plane," Steel says, and I swallow hard.

It'll be another week or so of travel, but this is it. I glance up at Steel, who stands on my left side. After training with Tor, I've been having lunch and long walks along the uppermost level of the ship with Steel. We usually end up in the ship's library, discussing histories I've never heard before, and then... well, I end up on one of the study tables while Steel devours me.

It's a good life, I can't deny that. Being able to satisfy my need to train right alongside my need to learn, and to have two exceptional males at my side while I do it. My heart aches at the secrets I've kept from my bonded mates, but I shove the pain down. I haven't told either of them about my trips at night down to Lock's cage. Even if I think they'll understand, they'd both likely try to protect me from Lock, and I don't need that.

I need answers, mostly from myself, but I need them all the same.

Talon is nowhere to be seen when the ship opens up, allowing us to venture down to the bustling city built at the base of the towering mountains. Once again, I'm in awe of the place. I've seen each realm—mine being water—Air, Fire, and now Earth. The elemental realms have opened my eyes to all the knowledge that was withheld in my studies, not to mention Steel's daily lessons with me. A gnawing sting splits my soul at the truth staring me in the face—there is no way my father didn't do that without intention. But for what? What does he gain by keeping me in the dark about the world?

He sharpened me into a weapon, an assassin hidden under a princess's clothes. But I haven't hidden my talents from my husbands, not since I'd needed those skills in the Fire Realm when Talon was nearly killed. And Tor and Steel have not suspected me or distrusted me since they learned I can wield ice into swords and daggers and spears.

My stomach churns. I was sent here to slide one of those icy weapons into their hearts or across their throats. And then do the same to the All Plane king when we arrived.

But after all I've learned? After all I've felt?

I'm not sure I have the strength to do it.

Especially when Steel and I have discussed at length how to integrate our two realms—slowly and with intention. His dreams are such beautiful dreams, and I want them to come true. I want them more than I want bloodshed. But I know my father, and he'll never bend the knee to the All Plane king.

All I've ever wanted for my people was freedom. For my father to loosen the restrictions he holds on them because of the threats to our realm. Though, after learning all I have, I now wonder if it was all a guise to keep our people in check. To keep them living in fear.

"Are you hungry, little wife?" Tor asks, drawing me to the blissful present. The sight before me is one of beauty, a peaceful people with glistening lavender skin, hunter-green eyes, and swishing tufted tails. Each is welcoming and they invite us to rest and relax before the last leg of our journey.

"Always," I answer, shaking off the darkness clinging to me. I'm running out of time. My father's will is strong in me, battling the bonds with each beat of my heart—his orders of *kill, kill, kill* like a pulse in my veins.

Kill for our people.

Kill for our land.

Kill the princes to free us all.

"Let's feed you then," Steel says, each brother taking one of my arms as they lead me deeper into the city.

I silence the battle in my head, my heart, and breathe in the crisp mountain air. The faint smell of snow sends tingles down my spine, reminding me of Lock. It's quickly whisked away by scents of roasted meat and fresh vegetables, sweet wines and pastries as we pass by shop after shop offering such goods.

This is our last stop. Our last chance to simply *be* with each other outside the ship before we make it to the All Plane. Terror spears me with that knowledge, and I decide not to waste this moment.

I grip Steel's and Tor's arms a bit more intensely, and they draw closer to me as we head to a restaurant with outdoor seating and a perfect view of the mountains. We're quickly ushered to a table, and the drinks and food flow. An endless supply for the princes and their new bride, all in gratitude for how much the royal family has done to keep their city safe.

Tor and Steel do as they normally do when praise and thanks come their way. They kindly accept it and hurriedly divert the conversation. They don't want me to continue to hear stories of the attacks coming from Shattered Isle soldiers. And while I denied it with a fire in my heart weeks ago, it's hard to dispute it anymore when every city we've docked in has recanted similar horror stories.

Shame threatens to coat my skin like an oil and I have the sudden urge to run back to the ship and hide outside Lock's cage. He knows what it feels like to be shamed and judged just for being what you're born as, and sure, he might be a monster, but apparently, being a Shattered Isler makes me one too. And I hate that I didn't know. Hate that I wasn't prepared for any of this. I came in here *knowing* the All Plane princes were the villains. Now it's becoming clear that my father raised me on horror stories of his own making—gruesome tales he credited to All Plane royalty.

"Eat," Tor says, sliding a plate of meat and greens and bread my way. He flashes me a knowing look, as if he can *feel* where my mind has wandered. Steel runs his hand over my thigh, loving and supportive.

I grin at them both and then dig into my food, using the actions to bury the conflict deep where the bonds can't feel the doubt, the worry, the fear.

By the time I've finished my second helping of food and a great deal of sparkling wine, I'm feeling more like myself.

"Dance with me?" I ask an hour later when music fills the air. The sunlight is giving way to night, and while I know we need to head back to the ship, the seductive notes call to my blood.

Tor and Steel share a glance as I rise from the table, as if they don't know who I'm asking. I laugh, the wine making bubbles burst beneath my skin. It feels amazing to be this free, this detached from the emotions I can't escape. But thanks to the wine? The weight on my chest lifts until I can breathe again.

I grab both their arms, tugging until they both smile at me and stand. I interlace my fingers in theirs as I lead the way to a wide space next to the restaurant where other patrons already dance.

The band sits off of the designated dance space, their string instruments looking handmade and intricately carved. I spin around once I've found a spot in the crowd big enough for the three of us and find Steel smiling down at me. He slides his hands to my hips, swaying to the beat of the music.

Tor's strong, broad chest kisses my back, and I glance up and over my shoulder at him as Steel moves closer. My skin ignites, and a flame licks my spine at the strength surrounding me. Tor's hands glide over my neck and shoulders, Steel's remain on my hips, and we move like one fluid movement to the melody.

The beat is slow and sultry with thick notes that spill over one another like heated honey. A steady, low beat pulses behind the string sounds, creating a tune so thriving with life I feel it expanding my lungs.

I swish my hips, grinding my ass over Tor's hips before rocking into Steel's front. I gasp at the contact, at the carved muscles that press and caress each soft part of my body. Steel moves a hand up, cupping my cheek before slanting his lips over mine. I open for him, relishing the feel of his tongue gliding over mine while we all still move to the music. He draws back, leaving me breathless and aching as he smirks at me.

A strong hand slides around my throat from behind, gently urging my head back. I tip my chin, glancing up and behind at Tor, who claims my mouth with a warrior's strength. I whimper from the intensity in it, from the way our bodies are still connected in the dance. I'm like a struck match and their kisses are the gasoline.

Tor nips at my bottom lip as he draws back, and a warm shiver races down my spine as the song ends. The three of us stand there, chests heaving, as we silently share a conversation. Stay or go.

We need to go, each of us knows it, but of course, I want to stay in this moment forever. Want to stay lost in the music, sandwiched between them in this slice of calm before the storm.

"We should head back," Steel finally says, voice rough.

Tor nods his agreement, but neither of them moves until I say, "All right."

Night blankets the sky by the time we make it back on the ship. Both Tor and Steel walk me to my room. My body is a coiled spring, aching and begging for release by the time we make it to my door. The two bonds inside me are flickering with heat, twisting with the need to be stroked.

I swing my door open, spinning around when I don't hear anyone following me. I arch my brow at both Tor and Steel lingering in the doorway.

"Don't you want to come in?" I ask in a voice that sounds so much more confident than I've felt lately.

Again, they share a confused look, as if they don't know who I'm asking. And sure, we've all slept together, but never at the same time. But after that dance? I want *more*.

I want the warrior's lightning and the heart's passion.

I want to lose myself in my husbands, the bonds between us strung tight.

I want them both to consume me until there is nothing left in my mind but this new reality. One where I'm theirs and they are mine and nothing else in the universe matters beyond that.

Walking up to the door, looking up at them, I submit myself to that desire and give nothing else a bit of thought. My eyes widen as Talon pauses in the hallway behind them, glaring at us as if this display just seriously put him off course of wherever he was heading.

I slide my fingers over Tor's arm, then Steel's, and tug them both into the room, never taking my eyes off Talon's—which are as sharp as daggers. I arch a brow at him, but there is nothing but ice in his eyes, so I slam the door shut.

"I want more dancing," I say, and Tor chuckles.

Steel heads across my room, clicking something on one of the walls. Seconds later, similar music to what we just heard filters into my room, and I clap delightedly.

I sway to the music, arms extended for both of them. Tor is closest, so I face him, keeping up the movement in my hips as I reach for the buttons on his shirt. It's off in a blink, and I spin as I feel Steel behind me. I lift the hem of his shirt, and he tugs it off the rest of the way, tossing it behind him.

I sigh at the sight of them both, all smooth skin over gobs of corded muscle, and I trail my fingers over them both, grinning as we fall into an effortless rhythm to the music.

Steel's fingers tease the skin beneath my shirt before he lifts it up, freeing me in one smooth motion. The cool air hits my bare breasts, but Steel's hands are there, cupping them in his hands as we all continue to dance. He pinches my nipples until they're tight for him, and I tremble as he lowers his head, smoothing his tongue over each one.

Tor grips my hips, rotating me so my back is at his chest again, giving his brother more access to my breasts. A moan escapes my throat as Steel sucks a nipple, then swirls his tongue around it. I arch into his teasing, the motion causing my ass to brush over Tor's hardening cock.

A lick of awareness flares through me as Tor hooks his fingers into the band of my pants and yanks them down. I step out of them and reach for Steel's pants as Tor takes care of his own. And then there we are, completely bare for each other, my body the only space between the two glorious males as we dance in the muted light of my room.

The heat from their skin teases my own, and I can't stop myself from reaching for Steel's hard cock, pumping it as I roll my ass over Tor's. Teasing, flirting, nothing more than a torturous little dance. Steel claims my mouth with a growl, and I squeeze him harder. Tor glides his hands over my hips, sending one around and down to the apex of my thighs. He groans at the slickness he finds there, gliding his fingers straight through the heat of me.

I jerk my head away from Steel's kiss, gasping as I tip my head back against Tor's chest, completely at the mercy of those damn fingers. He grins down at me, swirling his finger around that bundle of nerves that begs for more pressure.

Steel grips my chin, forcing me to look at him before taking my mouth again. I pump him, relishing the feel of velvet-covered steel in my hand as Tor tortures me with his. My mind whirls with the sensations, each nerve ending in my body sparking to life in a way I've never experienced before.

These two.

Always taking me to new heights, and tonight? I want to take everything they give and give everything back in return.

Tor slips a finger inside me, then two, pumping hard and fast. I forget we're dancing, forget the music thrumming around us, forget everything outside the feel of his fingers pushing me toward that sweet, sweet edge. Steel teases his tongue along the edges of my teeth, and I moan as I rock into Tor's hand.

Steel backs up enough that his cock slips from my grip, and I stare at him accusingly for all of two seconds before his mouth is on my breasts again. I gasp as he tongues my nipples, and Tor increases his pace. My knees tremble from the effort it takes to keep upright, and I lean on Tor's chest for support. He kisses my neck, biting down as he presses the heel of his palm flat against that aching bundle of nerves. Steel flicks his tongue, and everything inside me unravels in one burst of sparkling energy.

My body shakes from the orgasm as I keep rocking against Tor's hand, keep arching my breasts into Steel's mouth until I go limp from the intensity of it.

Tor must feel it because he gently guides his hand out of me, spinning me before tossing me over his shoulder like I'm nothing more than a doll. I laugh, not bothering to fight him as he carries me toward the bed. He sets me on my feet before it, taking a seat on the edge of it himself before spinning me once again.

I look at him over my shoulder, my eyes flickering between him and Steel, who stalks across the room to stand before me. My heart races against my chest, my skin flooding with heat. I've never done this before, and I'm suddenly at a loss on how to make this all work.

"What do you want me to do?" I ask Tor, my voice breathless.

He grins up at me, lightning crackling in his eyes and on his fingertips as he grips my hip. "Sit that pretty little pussy on my cock," he demands, tugging on my hips.

Electricity flares through me in delicious tingles, and I do as he says, situating him at my center and slowly sinking down. I moan at the feel of him inside me, and he instantly wraps an arm around my waist, holding me in place. My eyes are on Steel as he looks down at me, his glorious body on display in the muted lights in my room. This close, I can see every dip of his muscles over his abdomen.

"And you?" I ask, nothing but heat and anticipation in my tone. Does he want to watch and wait or—

"Open your mouth," he says, and my heart stutters, my pulse skittering as Tor moves beneath me. I tremble from the feel of him thrusting upward, his arm a band of iron around my waist as he drives into me.

I wet my lips, stifling another moan as Tor uses his free hand to explore my back, my neck, my breasts. Steel steps closer, a delicious grin on his lips before he's standing right in front of my face. I gasp at the sheer size of him, always surprised and never disappointed. I open my mouth, not waiting a second before wrapping my lips around his cock. I have to lean forward to do it, and the angle has Tor sliding in deeper with every thrust.

I moan around Steel's cock, and he hisses as I swirl my tongue around his head. I reach for him, gripping his hips as I urge him closer.

"Fuck," Steel groans as I take him deeper. My heart races in my chest, my body a buzzing string of pleasure as Tor continues to drive into me. Steel fills my mouth so much I can hardly breathe around him, but I relish the feeling—hang on every groan coming from his and Tor's chest.

Me.

I'm doing that to these two powerful, amazing males. I'm driving them mad with need. It floods my mind, and soon I'm lifting and dropping onto Tor's cock in the same rhythm that I bob my mouth on Steel's. Tor fills every inch of me, and tendrils of his lightning dance over my skin, sending shivers of pleasure and pain rocketing through me,

Our bonds flare brighter than the stars I adore, braiding and pulsing and purring. My muscles clench, and I moan around Steel's cock as Tor takes the reins again, driving into me so hard and fast the sounds of our bodies crashing together fill the room.

Steel winds his fingers through my hair, and I submit to him entirely as he fucks my mouth. Each thrust, each touch, creates an internal ball of fire that pulses and aches in my core. Tor shifts, driving into me long and hard while using his thumb to press down on my clit and I shatter into pieces around him.

I can't stifle my cries of pleasure, and each vibration rocks around Steel's cock as he fucks my mouth with a relentless sort of passion.

"Fuck," he groans, and moves to pull out, but I grip his hips and hold him there. "Cari, *fuck*." He spills into my mouth with a growl, and I swallow him down. Tor gives a final hard, intense thrust, his own release following mine as I tremble around him again and again.

"Fucking hell," Tor groans, his forehead falling to my spine.

Steel gently pulls out of my mouth, swiping his thumb across my swollen lips as he grins down at me. "You're incredible," he says, and a shiver races across my skin.

"Phenomenal," Tor adds, gently lifting me and settling me on the bed.

"You both are," I say, sliding to the middle of the bed, laying my head on one of the many pillows as I catch my breath.

Tor settles behind me, and Steel in front of me.

Tor slides his hand along my calf, up my thigh, and over my hip before starting the path over again.

Steel smooths back my hair, tracing the lines of my jaw, then my lips, and on to my neck.

They keep up their pawing until I can't help but smile at them both. "Again?"

Tor laughs, kissing my shoulder.

Steel cocks a brow at me, leaning in to claim a kiss. "It's only fair," he says. "I want to fuck your sweet little cunt this time," he says, his words sending tendrils of heat up my spine.

I grin at him. "I'm nothing if not fair."

* * *

Hours later, Steel and Tor sleep soundly in my oversized bed. I shift, silent as smoke, rising to my knees where I'm sandwiched between them.

They don't even stir at my movements, their chests rising and falling with a natural deep sleep rhythm.

My heart races against my chest as I fashion two daggers of gleaming ice in my hands, and inch them toward their throats.

This is it.

This is the moment I've been waiting for. These two immensely powerful males trust me enough to fall asleep in my bed, to leave themselves vulnerable to an attack.

Kill them, kill them, kill them. My father's voice echoes in my mind.

I used to think killing the All Plane princes would free my people of the "protective shackles" my father has made them live in…but now, I'm not certain of anything.

My fingers tremble around the icy hilts of my daggers, and bile crawls up my throat as I gaze down at Steel and Tor.

My mates.

My bonded partners.

Mine.

I shake my head, carefully climbing off the bed, and hurry to the bathing chamber. I toss my ice daggers into the sink and look at myself in the mirror, my eyes lingering on the evidence of Tor and Steel's hands on my skin. Heat dances inside me with the memory of both their hands on me, the taste of each of them, the feel of their bodies against mine.

My heart expands as my mind wanders to simple times with them, bantering with Tor or discussing future hopes with Steel. It's more than a bond, more than a friendship, and I realize with absolutely certainty…

I can't be the person my father wanted me to be.

I can't do what he ordered me to do.

And I'll have to figure out a way to deal with those consequences or pay for them with my life.

14
TALON

I turn the water temp up a few degrees past scalding, dipping my head beneath the steady stream. I press my palms flat against the marble wall, letting the heat blast some sense into my brain.

The look in Cari's eyes as my brothers followed her into her room.

The way lust churned in those depths, and an invitation lingered. For me.

Right before she slammed the door in my face. Fuck, even that act of defiance made me want to fuck it right out of her.

My cock hardens, and I blow out a tight breath.

Maybe I should've gone with cold water.

I spin around, letting the water assault my back. I rub my palms over my face, trying to get rid of my headache with sheer force. I wish I could blame the pain solely on our new bride, the irritatingly gorgeous and deadly female that I can't get a read on. But it's not all her. The closer we get to home, the higher my anxiety rises. An ache right behind my eyes, the same gnawing pain that consumes me when the solution to a problem is just out of reach.

I grab the soap and lather up a little rougher than necessary, hoping the motion might help jar an answer loose. My mind constantly races with scenarios old and new, a never-ending stream of thoughts and equations, problems and solutions.

But not for this.

Father will kill him.

The thought soars through my mind for the millionth time since we captured Lock, and the familiar stabbing pain in my chest ricochets through me, too.

I wish we hadn't found him.

I wish he'd never left us.

I wish he'd told me the truth about what he's been up to this past year.

I slam my fist against the wall. He's my *brother*. Regardless of what he's done, he's my *blood*. How can I hand him over to our father? He's been looking for a legal reason to execute Lock since his enchantment powers manifested. He won't hesitate to roast him on a spit the second we arrive home.

Which is exactly why I haven't told him we found him. I keep hoping the perfect solution will present itself to me, something that will spare my brother's life, but the answer evades me.

I close my eyes, rinsing my body.

It doesn't help that Cari haunts my every waking second and some of my sleeping ones, too. Fuck this uncompleted bond. I hate it. I hate her.

She saved your life.

She's *ruining* my life.

And my brothers... fuck. She has them wrapped around her delicate and deadly fingers.

Tonight had been proof of that. The sight of the three of them going into her bedchamber makes my blood boil.

They can't see it. See what she is beneath the looks and the questions and her fucking musical laugh. She's an assassin. A viper gifted and bonded to us to no doubt bring about our downfall. The Shattered Isle king has likely planned it since her birth.

She could've let you die. One down, three to go.

I growl, cursing my brain for always presenting every possible reasoning, deduction, and strategy. I can't deny that nagging question in the back of my mind. If she really was sent here to kill us, then why *did* she spare me? Letting the Corter kill me would've been so easy. All she had to do was sit there and watch him sever my head from my body.

But she didn't.

The *why* behind it irks me almost as much as her pleading eyes.

There's no way she's as innocent as she pretends to be.

And I'll prove it. Somehow, I'll find a way.

But I'm running out of time, and if *I'm* running out of time—if my suspicions are correct—then so is she.

* * *

The night sky blankets the windows of my ship, the interior lights auto-dimmed for the late hour.

I've slept little since the bonding ceremony and since capturing Lock. My hot shower did nothing to lull me into relaxation, so before I know what I'm doing, I start heading toward Lock's room.

Maybe if I explain to him how close we are to making it home and tell him what will happen to him, he'll let me in on whatever game he's playing. Hopefully, he'll tell me the truth. No more beating around the bush, no more secrets. I'll beg him if I have to. That's how much I want my brother to live… but I can't set him free if I don't understand his reasoning for everything he's done in the last year.

The murders he committed, the senseless violence against random cities across the realms…

Can he explain them away? Will he? Will there be any explanation that will suffice for me to cut him loose before our father gets ahold of him—

"Why do you want to see so bad, darling?" Lock's voice echoes through the hallways, and I freeze before rounding the corner that will take me to his chamber.

"I just…" Cari's voice trails off, and I curl my hands into fists.

So she leaves my brothers sleeping in her bed to come here? Why?

"You just, what?" Lock asks, his tone sharp.

Good. Maybe he can see through her, too.

"I need to know."

HER VILLAINS

Silence. The tension in my chest amps up, and I itch to stomp in there and demand what the hell she's doing down here, but I calm my nerves and wait.

"After all our chats," Lock says, and my eyebrows raise. She's been down here frequently? "After all we've shared," he continues, "*this* is the question you beg of me every time. I need to know. I need a good reason before I show you."

Show her *what*?

Cari's silence is like a weight on my chest.

"I think I know," Lock says, and I can hear him pacing, his coat scraping around his ankles. "But I'd rather hear you *say* it."

"Don't make me," she pleads, and my heart races so hard it almost hurts. Lock is a known chaotic, a powerful prince who went on a killing spree after he supposedly betrayed my father last year. How can she speak to him so fearlessly?

She's foolish. A damn beautiful fool.

A bang against the glass shatters the silence and Cari yelps.

"You *will* say it, or I won't give you the answers you seek." Lock's voice is terrifying, his power leaking into his tone. "I can always *make* you. You know that, don't you, darling? You know what I can do to your mind. Shall I start my own digging?"

"I need proof!" she snaps.

"Proof of what?"

A stuttered sigh shakes her words. "I just need to know the truth. I need a reason to not—"

She cuts herself short, and I hold my breath.

To not kill them.

I can practically taste the words she doesn't say.

Lock's silence urges her on.

"To not hate each of you."

"Liar," Lock says, and I wholeheartedly agree.

Anger rises in me like a tidal wave. If he's calling her a liar, then she certainly is one. Lock can enter people's minds, read them, shape them, twist them. And he has no reason to lie here, not when they both think they're alone.

I can't stand by silently anymore, not with his confirmation of her being a traitor. She didn't say the words, but she didn't have to. I can feel them across our forced yet uncompleted bond. And I'm fucking done.

Tor and Steel are asleep, and I'll make sure they stay busy in the morning. Lie to them if I have to. I'll do whatever it takes to save them.

"I knew it," I say as I storm around the corner.

Lock jolts in surprise, and Cari gasps as I grab her arm.

"Out for an evening stroll?" I practically growl as I yank her toward me. She yelps, tugging against my hold, but I'm too pissed off to let it register.

"You know the effect I have on women, brother," Lock says, eyes bright with intrigue at the struggle. "She can't help herself."

"Let me go," Cari says, but she can't break my grasp.

"I see you," I say, my tone lethally low. "I've seen you since day one." I storm over to the control panel next to Lock's room, dragging her along with me. "You like to play with fire, kitten?" I punch in the codes to open Lock's door. "You fucking got it."

I glare at Lock, who raises his hands and backs up a few steps.

The glass door slides open with a *whish*, and I throw Cari into the room so hard she stumbles over one of Lock's chairs, falling on her ass with a thud. I hurry to enter the codes again, and the door slams home.

My chest rises and falls as I glare at her, her eyes wide and accusing as she remains on the floor.

"Do whatever you want with her," I spit at Lock. "Just make sure there's nothing left to be used against us when you're done."

Something like true shock flickers in Lock's eyes for the briefest of moments before pure mischief replaces it.

I can't catch my breath, and my blood is pulsing hot in my veins as I whirl around.

"Talon!" Cari screams at my back, and I pause, something like regret stopping my retreat—a heavy, gritty sort of feeling that calls me a bastard for what I've just done. For what I know Lock will do to her.

But it's not enough to make me turn around.

To undo what I did.

So, I keep walking

And try like hell to ignore the sounds of her fists hitting the glass.

15
CARI

My fists hit the glass, ice spiderwebbing over it. Adrenaline races through my veins, my senses on high alert.

Every instinct roars at me to run or fight.

Talon disappears around the corner, my screams going unanswered.

My entire body shakes when I turn around.

He's there, standing over me, *towering* over me with his height, his black hair falling around his face as he looks down at me with narrowed eyes. There is such chaos in those eyes, the same alluring, dangerous call that had me coming down here every night.

But the friendliness I saw before is nowhere to be seen.

The male staring at me right now? *This* is the chaotic prince, the villain of legend, the one who has struck fear in everyone across the realms.

Ice kisses my palms, and I finally realize how disadvantageous my position on the floor is. If I'm going to survive, I need to get to my feet. Now.

I dart up, my eyes scanning every inch of his spacious cage, looking for a high ground—

His hand grips my throat faster than a striking snake. "You're trembling, darling," he says, his voice smooth as silk. I grab his wrist, but the pressure at my throat isn't enough to hurt, only enough to hold. He hisses at the ice I send around his wrist, but he doesn't let me go. His eyes gutter and a bolt of heat goes straight through our uncompleted bond. He leans in close. "You're not afraid of me, are you?" he whispers.

I raise my brows at him, looking from him to the hand at my throat and back.

The intrigue in his eyes disappears, and he glares at me. "You're going to get everything you asked for, darling," he says, yanking me in close enough to kiss. But he doesn't, he merely pins me with that cold stare. "But you're not going to like this. Not one bit."

Panic flares at the base of my spine, and I struggle against the hold again, but he brings his other hand up to my cheek—

A sweep of smoke and fog swirls in my mind, blotting out him, his cage, *everything*.

I can no longer feel the plush rug under my feet or his strong, callused fingers at my neck.

My body is weightless before a hook yanks at the pit of my stomach, hauling me down, down, down.

I slam into the ground, black sand bursting all around me from my impact. I feel the fall in my bones and scramble to my feet.

The midnight ocean sings behind me, and I whirl around. The Shattered Isle moons sparkle off the dark water, making it look like a moving onyx sky scattered with stars. My heart pounds against my chest as I lean down, raking my fingers through the sand.

Home.

I'm home.

"I'm pleased to see you've brought your royal council and highest regarded soldiers and guards."

The blood in my veins freezes at the sound of that voice.

My father's voice.

I spin back around, my mind spinning with the scene.

My father stands in a cove just down the beach, the black rocks of our Shattered Isle arching above his head. He wears his black, star-covered armor, and his dark blue skin has way less wrinkles than I remember. And there, before him, is the All Plane king standing in all his golden glory with a mass of warriors behind him.

"But I'm most honored to meet your gorgeous queen," Father continues, dipping low at the waist as he kisses the back of a beautiful female's hand. She stands next to the All Plane king, her golden skin practically glowing despite night blanketing everything. "And your eldest." He looks down at a boy who sticks close to his mother's side.

I study the child, who can't be any more than six. He has intelligent, calculating eyes, and he looks somewhat familiar.

"We're honored to receive your request, Shattered King," the All Plane king says.

"Please," Father says. "Call me Jerrick."

I gape at the friendly way my father is speaking to the king, someone he told me was a monster my whole life. I blink, slightly disoriented as I move closer. I hold my breath, daring to move into their view in that little cove, but they don't even blink at my presence. I step between them, standing on my father's right, and reach out my hand to touch his arm.

My fingers go through him like I'm a ghost.

"Call me Augustus, then," the All Plane king says.

Father dips his head toward the queen again. "You just had your fourth son, correct?"

The woman dips her head. "I keep trying for a daughter," she says, her voice soft and graceful.

"And where is your queen?" Augustus asks, eying the vast cove behind my father. "I thought we were supposed to meet her here as well. Isn't she with child?"

"Yes," he says. "Our first."

My heart clenches in my chest at the prideful look in my father's eyes. His first and last. Thanks to the All Plane king. I glare at him, at the way he so casually looks at my father, knowing what I know of him. What he'll do once I'm born. Slaughter my mother while my father is away battling the All Plane army, soaking our beaches in blood.

"Children are such a blessing," Augustus says, glancing down at the boy. He smiles up at his father. "No matter if they're born under the sun or the moon."

Father nods.

"I know my own queen is dying to meet yours," Augustus says. "Shall we retire to the palace?" he asks. "Our journey has been long." He motions to the sky ship resting on a flat piece of beach just off the cove. "And we're not as used to the night hours as you. Can we retire and iron out alliances in the morning?"

I glance up at my father, my heart racing.

I *know* this story.

This is where the All Plane king will betray us. He tries to kill my father before contracts and peace terms can be set. A trap. A ploy to take over our territory. The breath stalls in my lungs as the moment in time seems to stretch forever, as I wait for the traitorous blow—

One of my father's guards runs up from behind him, having used the tunnels of this sacred cove that connect to the palace farther inland. He whispers something in my father's ear, something I can't make out. A viscous smile twists his mouth as he nods at the guard. A dozen more warriors come to join the first.

"Jerrick?" Augustus asks, stepping just slightly in front of his queen and son.

"We can't retire to the palace," my father says, drawing out his longsword from the hilt at his hip.

The All Plane guards behind the king draw their weapons instantly, as do my father's guards. Augustus shoves his queen and son behind him.

"What are you doing?" the king asks, drawing his own weapon, a spear of gold tipped with deadly points on both ends.

"Keeping you here," my father says. "While my armies raid your unprotected realm."

My stomach hits the beach at my feet.

"What? Why?" Augustus moves as my father moves, the two circling each other as the queen and son are herded back into the circle of All Plane guards. "We're supposed to be allies now. You and I are changing the course of history—"

"There is no such thing as peace," my father spits. "Only power and blood. And your kind has taken too much of ours in the past."

"Our *fathers*," Augustus growls. "We can change. We can undo the damage they did."

"No," father says, raising his sword. "The only change to come is your head on my wall, and my people taking your realm for their own."

Panic claws up my spine, but I'm frozen.

Father raises his sword, Augustus raising his spear in defense, but father sends his blade soaring over the king's head.

A feminine cry splits the air, and I watch in horror as my father's blade sinks into the queen's chest. The boy tries to catch her as she falls backward, but he's not strong enough.

Augustus roars, shoving his spear toward my father's neck. A guard blocks it, shoving the king back.

The boy is crying at his mother's side, a slew of All Plane guards hauling away her limp body and racing her back to the sky ship. He grabs one of the guards' swords, his little hands barely able to hold onto the hilt as he charges for my father.

A guard snatches him up, throwing him over his shoulder as he runs for the ship. The rest of the guards are in an all-out brawl, steel clanking against steel, blood and screams and sweat suffocating the space around us.

One tosses my father another sword, and he clashes it against Augustus's spear. The two are all teeth and snarls, looking animalistic as they battle in the sand.

"You will die tonight," Father says, swiping that sword near the king's head. "So will your sons, so your line will no longer draw breath. And know that each and every one of the All Plane that doesn't bow to my rein will die right alongside you."

"Heartless, *evil* bastard." Augustus slashes that spear through the air, the tip grazing my father's cheek and drawing blood. "Everyone advised me against aligning with you. Said Shattered Islers couldn't be trusted. But I defended you! I said we were both more than our father's mistakes!" Another swipe, another clash of steel. "We were supposed to be the change for our children!"

"You're a fool," Father spits, shoving him back with a huge blow.

Augustus stumbles backward, spear still in hand. His eyes flash to his guards, his council lying dead on the beach. All but the two who took the queen's body and the prince to the ship. The two who are racing back for their king now.

Father lunges, his sword sinking deep into the king's thigh. Augustus snaps the spear, breaking it in two. He shoves both ends into my father's shoulders, aiming for his neck but missing.

The roar my father unleashes is harrowing, and the All Plane guards grab the king, despite his protests, and haul him back to the sky ship.

"You will regret this!" Augustus calls, and my father sinks to his knees as blood spills from his wounds.

The scene wobbles around me, and I can't catch my breath, even as that hook in my stomach tugs me backward so fast my vision blurs.

I don't fall to the ground this time.

I hover in the sky as if I'm a spectator in a dream.

No, a *nightmare*.

Because that's what this is.

A clash of thousands of soldiers, both All Plane and Shattered Isle, erupts below me. The screams rake against my bones, the smell of blood sickening my stomach. But…it's not on Shattered Isle beaches, but golden sands of the All Plane.

Tears prick my eyes, my lungs aching.

Father told me the great battle happened when the All Plane warriors invaded our territory to claim it. He told me the king himself had snuck into our palace while the battle raged and killed my mother in her sleep.

But the king is here, amongst his men, battling and hacking away with pure hatred in his eyes.

"Vengeance is an ugly thing, isn't it?" Lock's voice is all at once everywhere, echoing from the depths of my mind.

Tears roll down my cheeks. I can't tear my eyes away from the scene. Father is nowhere to be seen. And even though I was just an infant, somehow I *know* he's in the stronghold of the palace, protected. Guarded.

"The Shattered Isle king's betrayal is what provoked this battle," Lock continues, his tone saddened. "And Talon," he says. "He never got over the brutal murder of our mother."

Talon.

The boy.

By the night, the boy had been *Talon*. He'd seen what my father did to his mother. No wonder he hates me. It's a marvel they all don't. Are Steel and Tor pretending? Are they using me the way I'd been raised to use them?

My stomach churns.

So much blood.

So much death.

Senseless, horrific death.

And all this time, I believed it was *them* who invaded our island.

Them who drew first blood because they hated our traditions, our culture.

Them who killed my mother—

"The date?" I ask, my voice hoarse, as if I've been screaming.

"The twenty-fifth day on the fourth month. Two hundred years ago," he says, and my blood runs cold.

"I wasn't even born yet," I say.

"No," he says, the battle still raging on below. "You're born days later. After my father's armies win and yours surrenders." Shock ripples through me. "The terms of the agreement were set in exchange for no more blood to be spilled. The Shattered Isle is cut off from the All Plane realm, and other realms too, though your father eventually got around the last rule."

I barely register his words, my mind whirling with the truth before me. And I *know* it's the truth, can feel it in my bones. Can smell it in the air. Sense it in the devastation in Lock's voice. Can feel it along that uncompleted bond of ours.

"My mother," I say.

"I only know what my father told me," he admits. "He wasn't there to witness her death, so I cannot show you."

"Tell me."

"Childbirth," he says, and I cave in on myself.

"I've seen enough," I say through my tears.

The scene dissolves into glittering black dust, and I'm yanked back.

I jerk at the sensation, my head smacking back against a chair.

I'm sitting in Lock's chair.

I blink a few times, swiping at the tears on my cheeks. I tuck my knees up, wrapping my arms around them. Two hundred years—the length of time it takes us to fully mature into our powers—and father lied to me every single night.

"I warned you," Lock says, and I jolt at the nearness of his voice—no longer in my mind but right behind me. It's only when he slides his hand off my shoulder that I realize he was still touching me.

He rounds the chair, slumping into the seat across from mine, his massive frame taking over the armless chair.

I glance at the place he'd been touching, my brow furrowing at how we went from him gripping my throat to me sitting comfortably in a chair with his hand on my shoulder.

Lock shrugs, his eyes still drenched in regret and sadness. "It strengthens the enchantment if I'm touching the person."

I focus a glare on him, uncurling myself as I sit up straight. "That...you didn't lie to me."

He glares right back. "Now, why would I lie when the story is so gruesome all on its own?"

I flinch but tilt my head at the spark in his eyes. At the way he's trying so damn hard to sell that excitement, try to make me believe he *lives* for that kind of bloodshed. But I heard his voice in my mind during the memory—his father's memory. I felt his anguish down that weak bond of ours.

He does not relish this, no matter what he wants people to believe.

My instincts flare back to life when he shifts in his seat, draping an ankle over his knee. He smirks slightly at the sight of me drawing back, going on the defensive.

I'm in Lock's cage.

And with what he's just shown me?

It changes everything.

16
LOCK

"You could've lied," she says again, her face still shaped with shock and anguish and a good deal of rage.

"Yes," I say, smoothing out my jacket. Doing anything with my hands that doesn't involve touching her again.

"But you didn't."

"No." I didn't mean the response to come out as a growl. But with her so close? That once mere flicker of a bond is demanding attention. We've spent countless nights speaking with a pane of glass separating us, and now?

She's *here*.

Talon threw her in here with *me*.

And he expected me to do such horrible things to her. To torture her for information—and fair, I've been known to do that, to delight in it—but he didn't stop there. He'd basically given me free rein to reshape her mind. Spin her into a walking drone if I saw fit.

Power is an intoxicating thing. I've seen it work like a poison, especially in my father. He once may have been a good man —from the memories I saw in his mind—but *I've* never known him as one in my two hundred plus years.

"You could've shown me anything. Taken me anywhere. Why, Lock? Why show me the truth?"

"Always so many questions with you," I say, pinching the bridge of my nose.

"It's our game," she says, and my muscles ache with the need to touch her.

She figured me out so quickly. That first night she visited my cage. She saw the luxurious trap for what it was—a prison. And she knew the only way to get me to talk was to offer up personal details of her own. Quid pro quo. And yet, she still didn't realize who really held the power between us.

"Would you have preferred I show you your deepest, darkest fears?" I ask, leaning forward slightly, almost as if a magnet is pulling me toward her. I may not have been at the bonding ceremony, but the priestess made damn sure to include each All Plane prince in the vows. I can feel that band of connection tugging tight between us, *begging* us to complete it.

Fuck, it's no wonder Steel and Tor caved so easily.

How the hell has Talon resisted so long?

Well, I'm stronger than him, certainly.

I reach out with my mental powers, sliding into her mind like smoke under a door. She jolts a little in her seat, her eyes glazing over the way everyone's does when I enter. I blow out a breath, steeling myself against her essence. This is the third time I've visited her mind, and each time it's an effort to hold my will over hers. It's as if the bond between us gives her the ability to talk back, to shape the enchantment right alongside me, and that's never happened before.

She doesn't fight me, just as she didn't when I showed her my father's memories of how The Great War started. Gave her the answers she so desperately needed.

I curl my fingers, using the physical motion to help propel my mental powers as I traipse about her mind. There are so many beautiful onyx caverns in here—no, *coves*. They're coves from her beloved Shattered Isle. Her mind is full of these precious pockets of memory, each one ripe for the plucking. I turn, randomly stepping into one—

"Pathetic," her father's voice rings across the training room.

Cari looks no more than ten years old. She's on her back in a wide circle of black sand. Four fully grown men wearing Shattered Isle guard armor stand over her, blades poised at her throat.

"Again," the king commands.

The guards back up a few paces, one kicking a wooden blade no bigger than her hand toward her.

She scoops it up, wiping blood from her nose with the back of her hand. Her long, black hair blows in the wind as the dark ocean rages behind her, the stars sparkling in the sky.

"I'll do better, father," she says, her eyes seeking him, his approval.

He tips his chin up at her from where he sits atop the arch of one of those coves. "See that you do, daughter."

A guard lunges for her, and she deflects his attack with the tiny wooden blade, but just barely. Another swipes her legs from beneath her, and she cries out when another drags his blade over her arm—

Rage ripples through me like an ocean current, and I snap back to the present.

She heaves a breath from the force of my retreat, and a low snarl slips past my lips.

"That's not your worst fear," I growl.

"You don't know a thing about me or my fears," she snaps back.

"Don't I?" I challenge. "We've spent a great deal of time together these past weeks. I know that you can't hear music without dancing. I know your favorite sound is the ocean at midnight. I know that you're a trained warrior but don't relish killing unless in defense." Her chin tips up in defiance, but she doesn't deny anything I say. "And I know that you're questioning everything right now, down to the very things that make you *you*, and it has you so desperate that you've retreated to my cage every single night searching for truths you weren't prepared to uncover."

She glares at me as she folds her arms over her chest. The motion draws my gaze over her breasts straining against her silk nightshirt.

"Fine," she relents, blowing out a breath. "You know me. But you still don't know a thing about my fear."

Oh, she has no idea.

"Failure? Disappointing your father?" I chide her, recalling the memory I'd walked into. "You're better than that." I lean farther forward in my seat, so close my knee brushes hers.

She doesn't jerk back. Doesn't curl her lips in disgust. Instead, she holds my gaze. A warrior princess on the verge of becoming a queen. There is fear in her eyes, but there's more excitement and wonder than that.

A distraction, no doubt. To stop me from digging too deep. But it's too late for all that. I have her here, and she's mine for as long as Talon keeps Steel and Tor away, and I will not waste one second longer *wondering* where her true loyalties lie.

I slide my hand over her bare knee, the white silk shorts she wears barely covering her luscious ass. Chills erupt under my touch, and her breath catches. I sigh. The feel of her dark blue skin beneath my fingers is the sweetest torture. It's been so long since someone hasn't cowered under my touch. Too long since I've reached for anyone with gentle hands instead of a killer's grip.

"Show me," I say, lowering my voice into that calming tone that sets people at ease. Her tense shoulders relax, her eyes glazing as I dive back into her mind. "Show me what you're terrified of, darling."

Black envelops me as the coves in her mind are slowly illuminated by moonlight. I can hear the ocean in the distance, her beloved Isle.

"Show me," I say again, walking faster past the coves. There are so many, her mind a vast and wonderous place. I want to spend hours, days, nights, exploring her mind. Learning what makes her laugh and smile and moan. But I can't want that. I'm not allowed that kind of happiness. "Your fear, Cari," I say, her name rolling off my tongue with persuasion.

I want to be wrong.

I want Talon to be wrong.

But for the life of me I can't recall a moment in our long lifetimes that he's ever been wrong about someone.

But Cari, she's different. She's not afraid of me. She came to me on her own. And my brothers, Steel and Tor, they adore her.

"*Cari,*" I lace her name with command, and I feel her finally let go. It's not a submission, but a challenge.

"I dare you," she whispers. "You yourself said you won't always like what you see."

Something like apprehension coils around my spine as a cove is lit up by a beam of moonlight. I steel myself and saunter inside, meeting her challenge with fire in my heart. No one has ever dared to speak to me like she does, and I fucking like it.

I touch the rough edge of the archway, the cove glistening from the black rock her Isle is known for. Rounding the corner, I expect to see her father—a terrifying king she wants to please, wants to make proud. I expect to see him punishing her for never being good enough, or at the very least, I expect to see her mother's death playing out before her eyes.

I stop cold as the bitter, brittle taste of fear stinks up the space.

Ice splinters in my veins as I fully step into the cove.

Into her worst fear.

"Tor," I gasp, racing to my brother's lifeless body. His throat is split open, his blood staining the silk sheets where he lays sprawled on a massive bed. "*Steel.*" Steel is next to him, face down, eyes open and glassy, a knife buried in the base of his skull. "Talon." He's there too, at the foot of the bed, his chest a butchered hunk of meat from being stabbed so many times.

The metallic tang of their blood taints in the air.

I swallow hard, tears biting the backs of my eyes. My brothers...my *brothers.*

A movement in the corner.

She steps out of the shadows.

Cari. A bloody ice-dagger in her hand, red splattered across her white silk pajamas. She crooks a blood-soaked finger at me, smirking—

I yank myself back, my breaths heaving as I shake off the fear, *her* fear. Rage coils inside my veins, adrenaline flooding my body as I fly off the chair. She's on her feet in seconds, her steps a bit wobbly as she retreats from my advance. I reach for her, and a dagger of pure ice whirls to existence in her palm.

I halt at the kiss of its sharp edge at my throat, my breathing so ragged it nearly slices my skin. She glares up at me, her eyes glistening with unshed tears, her brow furrowed. I slowly raise my hands. She turns, urging me around until *my* back is against the wall and that blade of ice is pressing harder against my skin.

Heat rushes through my veins at the anger in her eyes, the hesitance.

"Do it, then," I say, careful not to move. "You were sent here to do it, weren't you? A command by your father to kill us all?"

Her bottom lip trembles just a fraction. The bond between us blazes to life with how close she is, her body pressed against mine so she can hold that blade to my throat with a killer's expertise.

"I'm a monster," I say. "A villain. That's how you see me. Moreso than my brothers ever have or will be to you. So, do your worst." She doesn't know the truth. Doesn't know the reasoning behind my traitorous moves recently. The reasoning behind all the deaths. No one does. But if this is the way I must meet my end, so fucking be it.

Get it over with and release me of the burden I've borne alone for too long.

"You're not," she whispers, and her hand trembles. "If you're a monster, then I'm a monster. You *saw*. You saw what he wants me to do." Her words are breathless, and a tear slips down her cheek. "And after everything you showed me?" She tilts her head up, her eyes imploring. "I'm the villain in *your* story."

I can feel her resistance down our uncompleted bond. Can sense her anguish. Her revulsion at having her fear laid bare before me.

She doesn't want to do this.

She sees me.

Sees all of us, and has not cowered.

"*I* should be the one locked in this cell," she says, visibly swallowing. "Not you."

"You did not commit your father's crimes," I say carefully, and slowly I reach for her. "And you know why I'm in here."

Her eyes snap up to mine, searching. "You are not a senseless murderer, Lock," she says, and my body reacts to the way she says my name. Fuck, she's so close, with her blade digging into my skin, and still, I *want* her. Want to hear her screaming my name. "Everything you do or say has a purpose, and I've *felt* you in my mind. Whatever you did recently, the reason legends are rolling across the realms about your depravity, the reason why Talon locked you in here, you have a purpose. A damn good one, I'm sure. Not that you'd ever tell me. Or anyone. Easier to keep everyone at a distance, right? That way they can't hurt you?"

I glance down at the blade to my throat, then back to her eyes. "You're one to talk, darling," I say, and her eyes widen.

I hold that level of arrogant calm on the outside, because on the inside?

I'm crumbling.

My walls are shattering.

This female, she's…she's seen right through me. Even when my brothers believe the worst about me, she somehow sees what no one else can. Maybe she truly is the one. A bonded mate—such a rarity. Maybe together, she can help me put an end to the injustices I've been trying to correct all this time. But none of that can happen if she doesn't make the right choice. And I *have* to know what choice she'll make.

"Do it then," I say, urging her on. I move just enough that the blade breaks my skin, and she gasps at the sight of blood on my neck. Her hand trembles, then her entire body. She lets out a roar, and the blade of ice shatters to a thousand pieces on the floor.

"I can't," she says, sobbing. "I can't do it. I love them. And you're—"

I spin her so fast her words cut off. I gather a handful of her hair, jerking her head back as I press her chest against the wall she just had me pinned against. She struggles against my hold, and my blood heats at the fight in her. She *could* break my hold—I've seen in her mind the things she's survived—but she doesn't *want* to.

"Are you going kill me, Lock?" she asks, her eyes glancing over her shoulder. "Add another piece to this game you're playing alone?"

Fucking hell. How does she know? Why can't she see me as the realms do? As a cold-blooded, chaotic killer?

"What do you want?" she snaps, rocking back against me, but all she does is scrape her ass against my growing desire. She goes still, and I feel her reaction down the bond straining between us. "What do you want?" she asks again, but it comes out a whisper.

The blood is pounding in my veins as what I *need* to do and what I *want* to do war inside me. I lower my lips to her ear, just barely grazing the shell. "I want to hear you *beg*."

17
CARI

His words are a whisper against my ear, and my entire body narrows to the feel of him pressed against my backside, his fingers tight in my hair.

"For my life?" I ask, even though I can *feel* his desire rock hard against my ass. My heart pounds against my chest, my breasts pressed against the wall.

"For my cock," he says and tightens that grip in my hair, then roams his free hand down my neck, my back, his fingers too light in their exploration.

A whimper escapes my throat when he slips those fingers beneath my silk shirt, his callused hand flattening out over my stomach as he hauls me back against him. His teeth graze the shell of my ear, then down my neck before he bites down. I arch against him, the bolt of pain rippling down my spine as he soothes the hurt with his tongue.

He growls when I rock back against him again, my body desperate for more. He moves forward, pinning me in place on the wall again. I hiss from the cold metal seeping through my silk shirt.

"I can do anything I want to you right now," he says, and his words make me tremble. "I can have you any way I want and there is *nothing* you can do about it."

I try to shift my body, try to move so I can feel more of him, but it's no use. He's so much stronger than me, so much more powerful. I can't break his hold, and I'm not sure I'd even want to if I could. His scent washes over me, all snow and stars, and it makes my head spin.

The palm he has flattened on my stomach moves, teasing the hem of my silk pajama shorts. I whimper again as his strong fingers graze just beneath the band, only to circle to the back, teasing circles over the base of my spine.

"I can do this," he whispers as he tugs my shorts down, exposing my bare ass to him. "Mmm," he says, leaning back enough to look down at me. "I can do this," he says, and smacks his palm against my ass hard enough to sting. I arch back, the slap ricocheting along my bones and jolting my heart.

He smooths his hand over the hurt, then slides back up to the base of my spine again. "I can do this," he says, and I hold my breath as the tip of his finger traces from my spine and down the middle of my ass. My blood roars in my ears, my entire being sparking to life at the forbidden touch. "And this," he continues, tracing that line right down the center of me until he's found where I'm wet and aching for him. "Fuck," he hisses, and the hunger in that word has my skin tightening with need.

He teases my heat with his fingers, drawing them back up the center of my ass and down again, creating a trail of internal fire inside me.

"You're so wet for me, darling," he says at my ear, yanking my head back another inch. "How long have you been aching for me, hmm? Since you put the dagger to my throat? Or before?"

My mind races as his other hand keeps teasing me, gliding through my slickness and back again. Each pass has me arching, rocking backward, trying to get more of his touch. He tugs on my hair again, nipping at my neck.

"Before," I gasp, the tiny bits of pleasure and pain swirling together to steal my breath.

"Ahh," he says, his warm breath washing over the hurt on my neck. "How far before?"

I'm breathless, my nipples tight and aching as he presses me into that wall. His fingers poise right over where I'm slick and needy for him.

"Be a good girl," he says. "And answer me."

I arch back, trying like hell to get those fingers inside me. He draws back, his hand retreating toward my back again—

"Since I first saw you," I hurry to answer, and I can feel his smile against my neck. His hand grazes over my ass in a blink, and then he's there, plunging two fingers inside me, pumping and stroking that deep, aching spot.

I rock against him, relishing the feel of his expert fingers as he teases and tortures me. He glides his tongue down my neck, planting kisses over my shoulder, all while pumping me, stroking me, winding me up so tightly I know I'll break any moment.

The bond inside me coils and stretches, begging me to complete it, to bind myself to him and him to me. And the harder he pumps those fingers inside me, the closer I am to falling over that sweet, sharp edge.

"Fuck, *Cari*," he says, and a wave of liquid heat fills me at the way he says my name. Such hunger, such desperation.

His fingers go still inside me, just when he's brought me to the brink of exploding. I whimper from the jarring sensation, my eyes hazy as I look back at him. He wraps more of my hair around his fist until I'm arching so tightly against him I can barely move.

"I said," he says, sliding his fingers out of me and skirting his hand around my hip. "I want to hear you *beg.*"

He grazes his hand over my stomach and down between the apex of my thighs, just barely touching where he was moments ago. He draws back again, and I force out a huff of breath.

"Please," I say, my entire being a coiled string of need.

"Please, what?" he says at my ear, nudging his still booted foot between my ankles, and spreading them apart.

"Please, *Lock*," I say, my words aching and breathless. "I need you to make me come."

He shudders behind me. "You have no fucking idea," he growls as he slides his hand between my thighs again.

His fingers are back, fucking me so thoroughly I moan. Everything inside me twists into a hot knot, and then he scrapes a callused thumb over my ultra-sensitive clit, pressing down right where I need him.

And I shatter completely, his name a cry on my lips as my knees tremble from the force of my orgasm. He strokes me through the waves of it, kissing up and down my neck until my breathing has evened out.

He releases my hair, and I slowly, almost timidly, turn around to face him. He smirks down at me, drawing those fingers to his lips and sucking them into his mouth. "Delicious," he says, his eyes glimmering as he rakes them over my body. "But I think you can beg better than that," he teases.

I step out of my shorts, which are a pool of fabric at my ankles, and arch a brow at him. I run my fingers over his broad chest, the feel of the soft cotton of his shirt such a contrast to his long leather coat. I watch his gaze, questioning, as I peel the coat off of him and toss it on the chair beside us. He doesn't break my stare as he lets me undress him, all the while looking at me in wonder, as if he thinks I'll run for my life at any moment.

And maybe I should.

Maybe I'm wrong about him.

Maybe he's every bit the killer the legends claim.

But I'm not afraid of him. I need him on a level I've never known possible.

I trace my fingers over the cords of muscle beneath his skin, eying his impossibly gorgeous body when I've stripped him bare.

My mouth goes dry at the sight of his hard cock, the size of it as he stands there, looking down at me with nothing but male pride in his eyes. I flick my eyes back up to his. "Please," I say, adding an extra ounce of hunger to my tone. He wants me to beg? Fine. He's already proven he's worth begging for.

"Please, what?" he asks, his voice rough and raw and sending shivers across my skin.

I tug off my silk shirt, baring myself to him, and delight in the way his eyes devour my body. "Please," I say again, pressing my palm flat against his hard stomach, walking him back and back until his knees hit the armless chair he'd been sitting in before. I stand above him as he leans back in the chair, smirking up at me. "Do you want me, Lock?" I ask, needing to hear him say it as much as he needs me to beg for it.

His tongue darts out to wet his lips, his eyes searing every inch of my body as he looks me up and down. "What do you think?" He shifts his massive thighs, his hardening length fully on display.

I grin down at him, my heart racing against my chest. I lean closer, gripping the wing-backed chair as I boldly straddle his lap. His muscles tense beneath me as I situate myself over the head of his cock, my heat sliding over him as I teasingly rock back and forth.

"Cari," he groans, his hands flying to my hips as he tries to urge me to sink over him.

I resist, using all the strength I possess to keep myself just hovering over his tip. He growls, and I smirk at him, capturing his bottom lip with my teeth. He likes to play games, likes a bit of pain mixed with his pleasure? Well, so do I.

"You dangerous, devious princess," he says against my mouth. I slant my lips over his, and he opens for me, our tongues meeting as the kiss consumes us. He tastes like a dream, and I tremble from the way I'm teasing him and downright torturing myself.

Finally, I can't take one more second where we're not joined, and I go to sink on top of him.

But he stops me this time, his firm grip on my hips holding me right over the tip of his cock.

"Lock," I whimper. "Please," I beg, just like I know he wants me to. "Fuck me."

A slow, seductive smile shapes his lips, and he releases me. I sink onto his hard cock so fast a moan rips from my lips.

"No," he says, leaning back even more in his chair. "I'm going to watch *you* fuck yourself."

White-hot tendrils of heat spiral down my spine at his words, at the way his eyes are a challenge as he looks up at me. I tighten my grip on the back of the chair and rock against him, the sensation stealing the breath from my lungs. He's so big he fills every inch of me, my slickness hugging him so damn tight.

I do it again, never taking my eyes off him. A muscle in his jaw ticks, his eyes hooded as he holds my gaze as his hands rest on my thighs.

Again, faster this time. I lift myself up, almost letting him slide all the way out of me before sinking atop him again and again. Over and over, all while those dangerous eyes are on mine, grazing over my body like a caress as he watches me use him to get myself off.

The bond glows brightly between us, a pulsing beacon of need purring at our joining.

"You're almost there," he says, grinning up at me. "I can feel it."

He's not wrong. I'm careening toward the edge, propelling myself faster with each time I roll my hips over his. The way he's leaning back makes the angle that much deeper, and he's hitting every spot without even having to move. No, he's content to watch me unravel above him.

"Now," he demands. "Cari, fuck, you're beautiful," he says, and the last roll of my hips has me flying apart above him. The throes of it send shivers all along my body, and I moan his name when I come down, feeling him still rock hard inside me.

He moves finally, sliding those arms around my body to hold me to him. "Good girl," he says. "I needed to make sure you came at least twice before I have my way with you."

Shock flutters over my face. "This isn't you having your way with me?"

He laughs, the motion doing delicious things to where our bodies are connected. "Not even close," he says, then he cocks a brow at me.

And I can *feel* him there, his essence at the edge of my mind. A polite request this time instead of a downright invasion. I open for him, my heart, my soul, everything. I'm done hiding, done being afraid of my own desires. For better or worse, I'm giving into everything I never knew I wanted.

Sweet snow and star-scented smoke fills my mind, but my vision doesn't shift the scene before me.

"Where should I fuck you, darling?" he asks, and my lips part. "I can have you peak on a snowy mountaintop, can make you tremble on a sandy beach, or perhaps you'd enjoy me spreading you out on a banquet table to feast on you for hours."

My breath catches as what he's saying plays out in tempting images in my mind. Anticipation thrills through me, feeling his power snake around the two of us, ready to strike. He can take us anywhere, without ever leaving this cell. And in the back of my mind, I wonder how many times he's wooed females this way. Wondered if he's ever let anyone in so deeply before.

A light smack on my ass snaps me right back to the present, and I moan at the way he feels inside me when I rock into him from the spank.

"Never," he says. "The answer is never."

"Reading my mind?" I ask, breathless as his hands roam over my body in lazy, languid touches.

"It's not hard when you've invited me in, darling," he says, lowering his head and drawing one of my nipples into his mouth. I gasp from his bite, then moan at the way his tongue swirls around the peaked bud.

"The stars," I say, and he goes still beneath me. I look down at him, gliding my fingers into his long, dark hair. "Fuck me in the stars."

The luxurious cage we're in melts away until we're floating in a sea of starlight. A midnight curtain blankets every space around us, diamonds sparkling with white and blue and even flickers of red.

A shocked cry escapes my lips, and then I'm spinning, my back pressing against the velvety smoothness of this slice of midnight sky Lock has created for us.

And he's there, pressing my knees apart with his powerful hands, baring me to him as his gaze lingers on every inch of my body.

"Tell me you want this," he says, his voice ragged as he stalks up between my thighs. He looks glorious and god-like as he does it, the endless night sky behind him and beneath us. The very thing that has always been my escape, my safe haven when I was riddled with doubt. I'd spend hours staring up at the stars, feeling like I could be myself before them and no other. "Tell me you want to be bound to me forever, Cari," he says, his muscular arms finding a place on either side of my head. His cock lines up with my slick, hot entrance, but he pauses. "Because after *this*, there is no going back. You still don't know the truth about me. About what I plan to do."

A tiny bolt of fear races down my spine, but the bond aching between us shoos it away. I reach up, cupping his face in my hands. "I want this," I say, and his eyes gutter. "I want *you*, Lock."

He slides in an inch, slow and torturous. "Even if I'm the villain in your story?"

My heart stutters. The truth of everything that had been exposed earlier races back to grip me in fear. I tip my chin up, eyes on his. "If you are, then I am too," I say, leaning up just enough to graze my lips over his. "Because I'm yours." I kiss him again before pulling back. "And you're mine."

He shudders above me before plunging all the way inside me. I drop back, arching against him, sighing with the connection, with him fully giving himself over to me.

Lock thrusts deep and true, again and again, until the bond between us is braiding together in an unbreakable chain that burns white-hot.

I dig my nails into his back as he grabs my knee, pressing it up and out so he can fuck me harder, deeper. Every pump of his hips fills me so much I can't think or breathe around the sensations firing all across my body—all sparking need and sweetest relief.

And I don't dare close my eyes. I arch against him, the soft sky cradling me as if we were in a bed of silk. The midnight blanket is peppered with diamonds that stretch out all around us, as if we are truly the only two people in the universe. As if this, right here, between us, is the only thing that matters.

"Cari," he groans when I hook my other leg around his back and urge him faster, harder. I want to be consumed by this male, devoured by him. Want to hear him say my name again and again. Where so many people fear him, he's bending for *me.*

"Come with me, Lock," I downright demand, my body coiling tight and hot as he thrusts in again and again.

"Fuck, *Cari*," he says again, pistoning his hips as he feels me tighten around him. A rip of pleasure streaks through me, tendrils of heat exploding down the center of me. His own release follows, only lengthening the aftershocks of mine, and I hold him to me, cling to him as I fall apart over and over again. Shattering among the sea of stars until I'm nothing but scattered starlight around him.

18
STEEL

"I can't fucking believe Talon," I growl to Tor as we race toward Lock's cell.

"If she's harmed beyond recognition, he'll get my strongest bolt," Tor says as we stop before the glass doors.

Adrenaline courses through my veins as I scan the interior while Tor enters the code on the control panel to open the doors. Chairs are knocked over, some of Lock's books scattered across the rug. But no sign of Cari. I crane my head, desperate to see around the corner where I know Lock's bedchamber is.

Talon tried to lie to us this morning when Tor and I woke up in an empty bed. Tried to tell us Cari was exploring the library or the pools or any other far-off place in the ship. It had only taken us an hour to realize she wasn't in any of those places. He wouldn't tell me why he'd thrown her in here with Lock, but I didn't take enough time to beat the answer out of him, either.

Lock is my brother, and I love him. But he's on a path none of us can follow, a dark one riddled with bodies behind him. He broke our trust when he left without a word, and Cari's been in there with him all night?

The glass door slides open, and Tor and I are inside in seconds. The place is wrecked. Lock usually keeps his space annoyingly neat. A red-hot anger races over me.

We round the corner, bounding for his bedchamber—

Cari is standing naked in the corner, her wrists bound by a tight strip of silk that hangs from the ceiling. Lock is bare before her, dragging a dagger made of shadows down the center of her breasts. She arches into the touch, but I can't see anything beyond the red marks along her skin.

A bolt of lightning cracks the silence, and Lock flies across the room. Bands of blue-white lightning pin Lock's wrist to the wall, his shadow dagger disappearing.

"Tor!" Cari says, and I can't tell if she's angry or relieved.

I hurry over to her, immediately undoing the ties at her wrists. She slumps against me, like her body doesn't have enough strength to hold itself upright.

"What did you do to her?" I snap as I haul her into my arms and against my chest.

Lock is grinning...*grinning* despite being pinned to the wall by Tor's lightning. "Not nearly enough," he says. Exhaustion and lust and a hint of madness colors his eyes, and Cari shifts in my arms.

"Tor, stop it," she says, but her voice is weak.

Tor growls, fastening her with a look that demands an explanation.

And I want them too, but right now, I just want to get her as far away from here as possible.

"Steel, I'm fine," she says. "He didn't hurt me."

"Much," Lock says, smirking. He flinches when Tor increases his power.

"Your body begs to fucking differ," I say, and she straightens in my arms.

"Fun's over, darling," Lock says.

I turn my back on Lock, hurrying through his half-destroyed room and through the door before she can respond to him. Every cell in my body is straining against our bond, which is weak, exhausted, and definitely in fucking pain. She reaches over my shoulder as if she can make me go back with the motion.

Tor follows seconds later, grumbling that he's going to handle Talon. I nod to him, racing through the ship until we've reached my chamber.

"You're being dramatic," she says, and I gently lay her on the bed, planting her with a look that is anything but soft. She visibly swallows, her eyes pleading with me. "He didn't hurt me," she says.

I glare at her, my breath tangling around the unfamiliar sensation. I'm *angry* with her. With her denial, with her defense of him. Running my fingers over her still naked body, I linger over too many darkened patches to count—bite marks, shadow dagger lines as thin as spidersilk, thumb prints...

Chills erupt under my touch, and my cock swells in my pants. I growl, shaking off my need.

HER VILLAINS

"Stay," I demand as I hurry into my bathing chamber. I'm back in seconds with some healing salve I always keep stocked. "Did he invade your mind?" I ask, popping the lid on the tin and dipping my fingers into the gooey mixture.

"No," she says, her voice pitching as I smooth the eucalyptus-scented salve over her wounded skin. They're not extensive, I have to admit that. Hell, even I'd marked her delicate blue skin each time we'd fucked, but still. I didn't like that she'd been *thrown* into a cell with my slightly deranged brother.

"What happened?" I ask after taking a deep breath. I continue doctoring the wounds and do my best to ignore the way her breath catches at each gentle touch. Fuck, even when I'm angry with her, I want her.

Or maybe I'm not angry with her. I'm *terrified* for her. For what could've happened to her.

"Talon found me talking to Lock," she admits. I cock a brow at her, and she shrugs. "I couldn't sleep."

"Even after Tor and I thoroughly wore you out?"

She smiles at me. "I slept a little after that," she says. "But I woke up, and you two were sleeping and..." She shrugs. "I've been visiting Lock every night."

I pause on my work, my fingers stilling over a mark on her hip. "What?"

"I have," she says, unapologetic.

"Why?"

"To talk."

"You *talk*."

"Yes," she says. "It's a thing people do."

I give her a chiding look, returning to my work. "Fine, what do you talk about with him that you couldn't talk about with me? Or Tor?"

"The truth," she says, and I swallow around a knot in my throat.

She doesn't need to explain further. The truths myself and Tor had danced around too much when she asked us questions about The Great War, about the hate between our realms.

"And he told you. Without asking for anything in return?"

"No," she says, sighing as I smooth my hands over a welt on her thigh. "Not at first." Something like excitement lights up her eyes. "We just...talked. Interests, music, simple things."

I furrow my brow, focusing on a small bite mark near her breast. She arches into my touch, practically purring. My cock hardens another degree, and I grind my teeth together. "I didn't know my brother was capable of such small talk these days," I say.

"I feel like there's a lot you don't know about him," she says. "Especially with the walls you've put between him and the rest of you."

I slide my hands off her body, putting the lid back on the salve. "You've been with us a handful of weeks, and suddenly you're an expert on our family dynamics?"

"No, of course not," she says, and I sink onto the bed beside her. I pull the silk sheet up, draping it over her body. Partly because I can tell she's cold, but mainly because I can't keep looking at her naked in my bed without wanting to kiss every inch of her skin. Undo whatever had been done to her.

"But," she continues, "I have the advantage of being an outsider looking in."

"You aren't an outsider," I say, and she gives me a soft smile. I reach for her hand, sighing when she intertwines her fingers in mine.

"I can see things from a different perspective. All you three can see is the brother that betrayed you, that went as mad and chaotic as your father always said he would." I tilt my head at her, wondering what her point is. "None of you have bothered to ask him *why* he's done the things he's done."

I swallow hard. The betrayal of our own blood, from the brother I love so much… it wrecked me. Wrecked us all.

"And he told you his grand reasonings and schemes?"

"No," she says. "But I can feel him." She places her hand on her chest. "Just like I can feel you, Tor, even Talon." Her eyes flicker down, regret and pain churning there. "He's not what you think. Not even what I thought when I first saw him. He's not the monster your father and the realms paint him to be."

I blow out a breath, rubbing my palms over my face. "So he tells you some horrific truths and suddenly you decide to complete that bond?"

"Truths you and Tor kept from me—"

"To spare you the pain," I cut her off. "Haven't you been able to tell by now that the idea of you, my wife, my *mate*, in pain is abhorrent to me?"

She squeezes my hand, forcing me to look her in the eyes. Fuck, she's so damn beautiful with her long black hair draping over her shoulders, brushing the tips of her silk-covered breasts. "I know. I understand why you did it, Steel. But you have to understand, Lock didn't just tell me the truth, he *showed* me."

My eyebrows raise, shock rippling over me. Lock rarely gave anyone anything without a purpose, and taking her into his own mind like that? That was... unheard of. He's never even shown me or my brothers our father's memory of The Great War, despite us asking so many times over the years.

"And," she continues, "you need to understand that he didn't do a thing to me last night that *I* didn't want. Didn't beg for."

My jaw flexes as jealousy sweeps over me uncontrollably. She sits up, moving close enough to smooth her fingers over that muscle along my jaw.

"You can't be jealous of Lock," she says. "No more than you would be of Tor or Talon. And after what we did yesterday, I'm pretty sure you have none of those issues with Tor."

"That's different," I say.

"How?"

"I trust Tor and Talon. I know they'll take care of you."

She eyes me. "Talon wanted Lock to destroy my mind, wanted him to tear me to shreds.

That's why he threw me in there."

But Lock *didn't*. And I had to stop and take a breath to mull that over. After the rumors of Lock's ruthless killing spree since he defected from our realm, I wouldn't have put it past him to harm Cari out of spite. A way to hurt us where it counted... but I also knew that he *let* us capture him, I just never knew why. Lock is more powerful than all of us, and sure, it took all three of us to bring him in, but if he'd wanted to? He could've slipped into each of our minds and made us live out our worst nightmares.

But he didn't.

And that fact had been bothering me throughout this journey, not to mention I'd been bothered since the day he fled our realm. None of it added up. He loved to challenge Father, loved to speak his mind and go against some of the royal standards, but I'd never thought he would be capable of the killing spree he went on recently.

Bodies don't lie, though, and neither do the consistent stories from witnesses.

But why?

It's a question that has nagged me for days on end, and the closer we get to our realm, the more my chest grows tight.

Father will publicly slaughter him, and my gut twists with the thought. Lock—despite his faults—is my brother. The same one who taught me how to shield my mind from other mental attacks, the one who read me bedtime stories when I couldn't sleep. The one who without fail gave me the last bite of his dessert after every formal family dinner.

Now he'd bonded with Cari, our mate. All of that added up to something, a conclusion I couldn't yet see.

And Cari had purposely sought him out, had visited him many times. Her heart is good, despite the conditions she was raised in. Somehow, she became this beacon of love and justice and hope all rolled into one. If she saw Lock as a worthy mate, then perhaps there is hope for him yet.

Still, something prickled in the back of my mind, some piece of the puzzle that didn't fit correctly.

"What game are you playing at, Cari?" I ask. She knew full well seeking Lock out would rattle us. Did she intend that? Is that the goal she's had all along? To shake us up and tear us apart, as Talon has said from the start?

My chest aches with the thought. No, it can't be true. Cari may have had her reservations about us in the beginning, but we're bonded. Tor and I both have felt the goodness in her, the bright hope for the future...

Cari parts her lips, her eyes churning with something I can't place. "I..." She closes her mouth, tucking the sheets tighter around her body. Exhaustion settles over her features. I want to press her for answers. Want to peel back those layers she keeps hiding under, but my mate's needs come first. And right now, she needs rest.

"This conversation isn't over," I say, drawing up the heavier blanket and settling it over her body. She leans back into the pillows, gratefulness filling her eyes. "And you should talk to Talon," I say as I head toward the door. "This hatred between the two of you has to stop. If last night is any indication, it's going to kill you both if you don't work past it."

She gives me a small nod, and I have to force myself out the door. All I want to do is curl up next to her, hold her body against mine and uncover every secret she's keeping, but I can't do that to her. It's only been a few weeks for her as our wife, our mate, and after boding with Lock? I'm sure she's reeling even more. Still, I can't help but wonder if I've let my love blind me to the truth...

My mate may have more secrets than we can survive.

19
TALON

I halt my steps as I round the corner into my control room, fire licking up my veins.

"You can't stop being a traitor, can you?" I growl.

Cari jolts a little, spinning around to face me. She tries to swipe her hand across the screen on the main panel, tries to close what she's snooping through, but I snatch her wrist before she can.

I scan the files she's opened on three separate screens as she tries to tug her wrist free. One is a standard history of my father, the other is my ship's charted course, and the last is an encrypted file I've never seen before. Something that looks a hell of a lot like encoded messages to the Shattered Isle.

"What are you going to do, Talon?" she spits, yanking on her wrist again. This time, I let her go, because I'm still staring at that document, my brain itching to work past the security measures on it and reveal what's inside. "Toss me in with Lock again? Didn't work out like you planned last time."

That's enough to snap me back to the present, and I glare down at her. "I guess I'm the only one immune to your charms," I growl, even though it's a fucking lie.

Since the moment she stepped onto my ship, she's been my torment, my temptation, and my terror. The mating bond begs for completion, and by sheer force of will, I've resisted. Even as I've watched my brothers fall for her, felt their love for her grow with each passing day.

She moves to step around me, and I click a few buttons on the control panel, the main doorway sealing immediately. She whirls around, her eyes wide and spitting fire.

Good. She should know how it feels to be trapped in a room with someone who drives her to the point of madness. Because that's what she does to me every single day. I can't help but want her, can't help but wish I can experience the joy my brothers are reveling in, but I'm not them. I can't turn off my brain, can't stop the calculations that help me see past every defensive wall she's thrown up since coming to us.

She's hiding something. Something big. And I can't let my own desires impede protecting my family from her. I thought Lock would slash into her mind and spill all her secrets two days ago when I threw her in with him, but even he's fallen for her.

I nod toward the encrypted message on the screen. "What are you doing, Cari? Trying to get a message out to your father? Is he planning an ambush?"

She raises her chin, defiant.

I cross the room in two strides, gripping her arms. She gasps, glaring up at me. "Is that why you're here?" I ask. "Get close to us, learn about our secret forces, and report back to him so he can finally annihilate us like he's always wanted?"

It's been two hundred plus years, but the memory of the day he betrayed my father hurts every inch of my body. I can still feel the loss of my mother. The All Plane realm gifts us with long, youthful life, but one slip in the walls I've built to protect myself, and I'm that ten-year-old boy again, useless against the attack.

"Answer me!" I demand, when some war rages in her eyes.

"You're the All Plane genius, blessed with a powerful mind that can calculate and create anything," she snaps. "You should be able to see that I wasn't trying to send a message, but *open* one."

I tilt my head, my entire body shaking with adrenaline. Every piece of me is shredding, begging me to take care of my mate, not accuse her of treason, but I *can't*. I know I'm right in this, can see it in her eyes. She's hiding something that can ruin us all.

"You don't believe me," she says in an almost defeated tone.

"Why should I?" I draw her closer, my jaw clenching at the inescapable need to touch her.

Her shoulders sink, and she stops trying to break my hold. Something broken and raw colors her eyes, a look I've never seen before now.

"I can't do this anymore," she says, but her anger returns. And I can't help it, I like it. I like her better when she's spitting fire, not playing the defeated, wounded act. We both know she's not some simpering princess who needs saving. She's a warrior, a downright *assassin* with the way she fought the Corters who tried to kill me.

Something shifts in my mind, and I jolt like Tor's hit me with a bolt of lightning. "You are an assassin," I say, and she doesn't so much as flinch. "He trained you, raised you as one, didn't he?"

"From the moment I could hold a blade," she admits.

I feel like the floor is tilting beneath my feet, but my grip remains firm on her arms. "The marriage, the bonding ceremony..." The answers race through my mind at rapid speed, all likely scenarios leading toward one conclusion. "It was all so you could get close enough to kill us. Learn about our powers, work out our weak spots. No other assassin would ever make it past our guards, let alone our personal defenses..."

Tears coat her eyes, and my chest feels like an ax is lodged in its center.

She's the true villain.

And she's played my brothers for fools.

I slam her against the wall next to the control panel, and she winces from the impact. Not an inch of space separates us, and she's not even attempting to fight back. It's like she can feel my fury, my anger, and maybe through our fragile bond she can, but I don't fucking care.

"Aren't you going to deny it?" I ask, my voice lethally cold. I move one hand to her neck, squeezing just enough to show her she's completely at my mercy right now, and I don't have a lot to spare.

"No," she whispers, and two tears roll down her cheeks. She stares up at me with a pleading look in her eyes, and her answer is enough that I should crush her windpipe. I should snuff her out before she hurts me or my brothers, but something deep within me pauses.

Hesitates.

"You've had plenty of opportunities to kill us," I say. "Steel and Tor are putty in your hands. You even had access to Lock." My chest is aching, some part of me mourning her before I've even eliminated her. But I *have* to kill her, right? She's admitted that's what the Shattered Isle king sent her here to do. I can't allow her to… "You let me live," I say, astounded. "Why not let the Corters kill me? One less task for you to handle."

She shudders in my hold, and I press against her harder, hating that every inch of contact is the sweetest torture.

"I visualized your deaths," she says.

My grip tightens.

"I knew how easy it would be to slip an icy blade into each of your chests after I'd made it into your beds." She glares up at me. "I had every intention of killing you all before we arrived at the All Plane palace."

I cringe at the mental image of my brothers sprawled out in a bed of blood, betrayed by the female they'd fallen for. Our supposed mate.

"I was raised to *hate* you all. Born and bred on stories of your monstrosities." She sniffs, more tears sliding down her cheeks. "But then I *met* each of you, and you showed me the truth of the realms. The genuine history. Mine had been twisted, tainted, and sketched in a way to make me have nothing but disdain for your kind in my heart." She shook her head. "But that hatred bled away. Your brothers are the source of opening the infected wound. They cleansed it, and Lock... when he showed me the truth about the male my father is..." Her words trail off, and the knife in my chest twists.

She stiffens and, in a blink, breaks my hold on her neck. One second, she's in my grasp, and the next, an ice dagger is cold against my throat. Anger vibrates my body as I eye the blade, then her.

"I can't hurt them," she says, her face twisted in pain. "I *love* them. Unrestrained and unconditionally. Despite how hard I tried not to. I can't be the assassin my father raised me to be." She shakes her head, then takes a step away from me, dropping the ice dagger.

It clatters to the floor, and I'm on her again, my hand squeezing tighter around her throat with her admission. Something like relief washes over her eyes, as if unloading the weight of that secret is the best sensation regardless of her life hanging in the balance of my fingertips.

"Do what you have to," she says, her voice straining around my grip.

She broke my hold once, she could do it again. She could've shoved that dagger into my throat for sun's sake. But she didn't.

"I'm done hiding," she continues. "But after you kill me, decode that message. I've been looking for all the proof of my father's deceit, but while hunting, I found another traitor, and it's definitely not Lock."

"How am I supposed to trust a word that comes from your mouth now?" I yell, and she flinches.

"I have no more reason to lie to you, Talon. You hate me anyway. And I told you every dark, sordid truth about me.

How I was raised and what I was meant to do. You said it yourself, I could've let you die. I could've killed Tor and Steel when we were together the other night or any of the countless times we've been intimate together. But I *didn't*." She cringes like the thought is abhorrent to her. "And it's not because of our bonds, but because they're good males. Even Lock, regardless of what you think. I love them for the males they are, for the truth they brought to light, and for the way they accept me for exactly who I am, loving me back despite my obvious faults."

Her words slash at the iron walls around my heart. Tear and claw at them until I'm an exposed nerve, raw and aching. I search her eyes, getting lost in the truth and vulnerability there, the honesty and acceptance, even as death knocks on her door.

"And me," I say, my heart pounding against my chest. "Could you kill me?"

Her gaze sharpens, the picture of hatred and desire balancing on a knife's edge. "I want to throttle you ninety-eight percent of the time," she admits, her eyes dropping down to the knife. "But I won't."

"And what do you want the other two percent?" I ask.

Something hot flashes in her gaze, and it's enough to strip away the last defense I have around my heart.

"The other two," she says, drawing in a deeper breath now that I've loosened my grip on her throat. "The other two…" She moves closer, like a magnet drawn helpless to its other half. Her eyes flicker from my lips to my eyes and back again. And I let her move closer until nothing but a breath separates our mouths.

We hold each other there, my hand still at her throat, my thumb grazing over the sensitive part of her neck, making her tremble with something that definitely isn't fear.

She closes the distance, a determination in her eyes that says if this results in her death, then so fucking be it. And that defiance that is both submission and attack has me in fucking knots as her mouth crushes against mine.

Everything in my body comes alive at her kiss, and I yank her closer. I slant my mouth over hers, taking full control of the kiss, my hand still at her throat as I punish her lips with my own. Fuck, she tastes like a dream, and the breathy moan that escapes her at my harsh touch has my cock hard.

I tear my mouth away from hers, shoving her back against the wall again. There is nothing gentle between us—there never has been. We're clashing steel and searing fire.

Her eyes are wild with lust and need and a darkness that matches my own. Our hatred tangles and unravels at the same time. Our breaths are equally ragged as her eyes drop to the hand I still have firmly around her throat.

I squeeze a little harder, and her eyes widen as I draw her back to me, stopping her lips a breath away from me. "Forget everything before you stepped on my ship," I demand, and she shudders in my hold. "Forget what your father said, what he tasked you with. Forget that cage of a life he held you in." I tighten my grip, brandishing a kiss so hard and desperate she groans. "You belong to us now, to *me*. Do you understand me?"

She nods in my embrace, a sigh escaping her lips that is pure submission and relief.

"What about the rest?" she asks. "We haven't discussed—"

HER VILLAINS

I cut her off with another kiss, and she moans against my mouth. "Later," I growl, my entire being reaching out with one unflinching need.

The need to claim her.

The need to erase the darkness between us.

The need to fuck her so hard and good that I'm branded across her damn soul.

She gasps as I shove her toward the control center.

"Take off your clothes," I demand.

She doesn't hesitate to shed herself of the silk covering her.

"Now you," she fires back, and I smirk at the authority in her tone. She may yield her body to me, but her spirit will always be hers. And I'll make damn sure it stays that way. For a split second, anxiety claws up my throat at what we'll face when this is done. What consequences will she reap from not completing her father's task?

Later.

I'll deal with that later.

I tug my shirt over my head, my grin deepening at the way her eyes take in my body. I unhook my belt, sliding it out of my pants. I toss the pants aside, but hold on to the belt. Her eyes widen at my cock, and I take in her bare body, my eyes lingering over every faint scar and mark over her luscious blue skin. Some of the scars are fresher than others. I linger on the sprawl of ink on her arm.

"Turn around," I say, and she visibly swallows as she obeys.

My cock aches at the sight of her submission, at the way she bends over the console without me having to tell her to do so. Her ass is glorious and on full display, and I can't stop the itch to mark her skin for myself.

I fold the belt in half, snapping it as I stalk up behind her. "You want to be punished, don't you?" I ask, a grin shaping my lips as her breathing heightens.

I smooth my free hand over that perfect ass, my fingers trailing down the line of it before I find her center. Fuck, she's hot and wet for me already, and she arches greedily into my touch. I lean over her, planting kisses down her spine as I tease her wetness, circling my fingers over that sensitive spot at the apex of her thighs.

"Punished for what?" she asks, all too innocently, and I instantly draw my fingers away from her. She whimpers at the retreat but moans when I grab a fistful of her hair, tugging it back enough that she has to look up at me over her shoulder.

"You *know* what," I growl, crushing my mouth on hers. By the sun, this game we're playing has me fucking aching with need. I trail the tip of my leather belt down her back, eliciting a trail of chills wherever it touches. "You planned to kill me. Kill my brothers. You think that will go unchecked?" I bite her bottom lip hard enough to draw blood, and she arches back against me as she gasps. Her body reacts to every punishing touch I give her and begs for more.

And fuck me if it isn't the sexiest thing I've ever seen.

"Take what you need from me," she says. "You have no clue how strong I am. You can't break me, Talon."

I still at her words, heat shooting to every nerve ending I possess. Fuck, maybe this female really is made for me. Because how else can she so quickly see through to the heart of me? To understand my dark desires and not cower from them? To challenge me and submit to me so willingly?

"We'll see about that," I whisper in her ear, and she pushes back against me again, desperate for my touch.

I lean back, releasing her hair and sliding my free hand to her hip. I draw the belt away before bringing it down on her beautiful ass. She gasps, a moan of pain and pleasure filling the surrounding air. A mark of darkened skin appears, and I look her over to make sure she's okay.

"Do it again," she begs, and I almost come undone from that plea alone.

I do it again, smacking the other cheek this time, relishing the way her back arches from the mixture of pleasure and pain. And she takes it, begs for it, matching my needs in every way.

A few more times, and she's rubbing her thighs together, desperate for contact. I toss the belt aside, dropping to my knees behind her, smoothing my hands over the marks I created. I trail my tongue over the sensitive flesh, and she sighs as I soothe every hurt I delivered.

"Talon," she begs, and I smile against her skin as I spin her around.

I grab her hips and lift her onto the console, a hiss escaping her from the cold of the metal. I drag her down so her ass is poised at the edge, and since I'm still on my knees, I'm in the perfect position to devour her.

I hook her knees over my shoulders, wasting no time as I set my mouth on her. She bows back, her fingers tangling in my hair as I feast on her. "Fuck," I growl against her swollen flesh. "You taste like dessert." I lick up her slit, drinking down her flavor.

She arches into my mouth, her grip on my hair tightening to the point of pain as she urges my face closer. I smile at her greediness, at her need for me as hungry as mine is for her, and unleash myself on her.

"Talon!" she gasps as I fuck her sweet pussy with my tongue. I draw back only slightly, sliding two fingers inside her and pumping relentlessly as I suck her clit into my mouth. Her thighs tighten around me as her breathing goes wild. A tremor racks her body as she comes apart with my name on her lips.

She tries to scoot back, but I lock my arm around her hips and force her down. Licking and fucking her until she comes again and again, her thighs going limp with exhaustion on my shoulders.

Only when I'm sated with her flavor do I plant a gentle kiss to my new favorite spot, and place her feet on the ground as I stand up. I grin down at her, loving the sheen of sweat glistening on her body and the hooded look in her eyes. She's lust-crazed and blissful, and as I step between her thighs, she looks like she might not be able to handle one more bout of pleasure.

Too. Fucking. Bad.

Now that we've crossed this line, there is no going back, and I'm going to show her exactly what it feels like to be my mate.

I slip my hand behind her neck, drawing her up so that she's chest to chest with me. I palm her breast with my other hand, rolling her nipple to harden it before sucking roughly on it. I do the same with the other, and she rocks her hips against me, the motion sliding my aching cock through her wetness. I stand up straight, claiming her mouth like I did her pussy as I line my cock up to her entrance. I draw back enough to catch her eyes, holding her in this moment of pure torture.

She wraps her arms around my neck, holding my gaze as she rocks forward, taking me to the hilt all on her own. I hiss, my jaw clenching at the feel of her around me. All hot and sweet and fucking perfect. Lava slides through my veins as I pull all the way out and slam home again, my body completely alive and on fire for the female in my arms.

I slide my hands around her back, holding her to me as close as possible as I pull out and thrust into her again.

And again.

And again.

Each time the lava in my blood strengthens, sliding out and around the bond between us. It gilds it like the rarest gold, strengthening it each time we slam together. Our bodies are merely vessels for the true pleasure, which is this bond curling and tightening between us.

Fuck, I've known nothing like it. Never experienced this level of pleasure in both the physical and internal before.

And of course, I haven't.

Because before I never had *her*.

My wife.

My mate.

Mine.

Cari captures my mouth as I pound into her, buttons beeping and screens flaring as I fuck her relentlessly on the console. But I don't care. Nothing exists outside of this feel of pure submission and joining. Nothing is as strong as this, nothing is as sweet as this.

She meets my every thrust with a rock of her hips, taking me as hard as she possibly can. Each pump is an eraser to the hate we shared. Each thrust a *fuck you* to the ax hanging over our heads.

And when she bites my lip while clawing at my back hard enough to hurt? I lose myself entirely. I piston my hips, fucking her hard and fast until I feel her clench around me. A flood of heat races down my spine as she comes apart again, and I follow her into that sweet abyss with my own release.

Our breaths are ragged as we cling to each other, our bodies slick with sweat. And I don't dare move, not while we come down from the sharpest high, wanting nothing and no one to steal this feeling from us.

But even as I hold her close, I know nothing lasts forever, and now that I've accepted her as mine? I'll fight to my last breath to hold on to her.

20
CARI

Talon carries my limp body to the shower in my room, where we stay until the water runs cold, the icy droplets enough to shock some strength back into my totally sated limbs.

"Will you get your brothers?" I ask as I slip into a pair of fresh clothes.

Talon slants his mouth over mine, the sting of his kiss sending heat straight through the center of me. "We'll meet you outside Lock's cell," he says, eying my swollen lips with a sense of male pride before he heads out of my room.

My heart races with the delicious burn of his touch lingering all over my body, and the newly completed bond pulsing brightly inside my soul.

There are four of them now, all unique to the male who owns it.

Steel's bond is a light of purest red and blue, a shield of resilience and compassion like I've never known.

Tor's is a white-hot light of blinding silver, crackling with energy and fun and lightning.

Lock's is a smoldering bond of the deepest green and gold, two sides of dark and light braiding together to make the most chaotic and passionate love I've ever experienced.

And Talon's? I never thought I'd see and feel what Talon's bond is, but I'm thanking every star in the sky now. It's an endless sea of ever-changing gears and spokes working together to create an unbreakable bond of iron.

I draw in a deep breath as I walk toward my door. With each bond shimmering endlessly inside me, and the truths I've learned over this journey, I walk confidently through the ship, knowing whatever comes, we'll face it together.

Still, worry creeps in as I find them all standing outside Lock's cell. Steel has his arms crossed over his chest as he leans against the opposite wall, his slick blue shirt making his eyes pop.

Tor tosses lightning between his hands as he arches a brow at me.

Talon has his hands in his pockets as he leans near Steel, and I can't stop the blush rising from my cheeks as I note he's put his belt back on. A thrill rushes through me at the memory of that belt on my skin, delighting me in the way he respected my strength and used the pain to give me so much pleasure I can barely walk straight now.

My eyes move to Lock, who stands near the glass doors, eying me suspiciously. My heart races at the sight of him as our bond flares brighter than the other three in that moment. I almost laugh to myself at the similarities between his desires and Talon's, and half wonder if I would survive if the three of us engaged in what Tor and Steel and I had before. For Steel and Tor were more alike in their tastes as well, and I wonder if we'd all been designed that way—bonded mates all working seamlessly to complement and satisfy and strengthen the other.

"You're a delicious little traitor, aren't you, darling?" Lock teases from where he stands, and his words roll over me like a hot wave.

"Talon filled you all in?" I ask, and there is a collective nod among the brothers.

For some reason, my eyes go to Steel's, and I suddenly realize it's *his* reaction I fear most. Not because I love him any more than the others—I love each of them for totally different reasons—but his heart is one of justice and fairness and compassion, and he may not be able to forgive me this slight.

Steel shifts off the wall, breaching the distance between us and scooping me up against his chest. Tears coat my eyes as he crushes me to him. "You could've told me," he whispers in my ear, and I melt into his embrace. He sets me on my feet again. "Did you think I would hurt you? Punish you for something so out of your control?"

My chest aches with relief, and I can't help but glance at Talon, who smirks at me. Finally, there is a peace between us, and it fills every hollow piece of me.

"I didn't know how to explain myself," I admit to all of them. "And now..." I shake my head. "Now I'm bringing a whole new set of problems to your door." The weight of that truth hits me square in the chest. "Honestly, you'd all be better off turning the ship around and taking me back to the Isle," I say, no longer feeling comfortable calling it my home. How could I when the entirety of my life had been shaped by lies? "You may be able to escape a conflict between the realms if you simply return me as unwanted goods."

Father will watch as his beloved second, General Payne, carves me up in front of him. I may have had my suspicions before, but I can no longer deny the monster my father truly is. Part of my heart breaks at that, but not as much as I would've guessed, which scares me even more.

But my people... they are innocent in this, most of them. I still need to free them from the fear my father has kept them chained with for far too long.

"Come now, darling," Lock says, and I turn to him, placing my hand on the glass where his rests. "You're not one to turn tail and run."

"Neither are you," I say, and his eyes bore into mine. There is so much there to unpack with him, but I know now is not the time.

"You're ours," Steel says, and I sigh.

"The only place you're going is home. With us," Tor adds.

I press my lips together, wondering how I got so lucky to be mated to such incredible males. My father underestimated how truly matched our bonds would be. We're true mates, an unbreakable unit sealed by fate, something Father couldn't have anticipated when he sent me here to kill them.

"Besides," Talon says. "We have bigger problems than your father to worry about."

We all shift our focus to him, and I nod at his questioning gaze. He's referring to the information I discovered before he found me.

"Our father," Talon says.

HER VILLAINS

Tor stops playing with lightning, Steel pushes off the wall to draw closer to Talon, and Lock merely says, "Finally."

"Explain," Steel says.

Talon looks at me. "Cari found an encrypted message before I stopped her..." His voice trails off, and a lick of heat travels down my spine. And standing here between the four of them? My desire is only amplified.

I force myself to focus, wondering about the rest of the specifics he found in that message. It had been buried among junk files, ones I sifted through to find some proof about my suspicions regarding my father.

Suspicions I found amplified after my night with Lock. After our mind sharing led me to a conclusion about his reasoning for killing who he killed recently, why he defected, and more. But I couldn't possibly tell the other brothers without proof, which is what I'd been searching for when Talon found me.

"I decoded it," he continues. "Along with about a dozen other messages that were hidden on a dummy server connected to the palace's primary system."

"You did all that in the time it took me to get dressed?" I ask.

"Are you shocked?" he asks, a smile on his lips. It's such a rare sight, it lights me up from the inside out.

"What did they say?" Tor asks, drawing us back to the point.

"That Father is a liar," Lock says in such an exasperated tone, as if he's astounded it took his brothers this long to figure it out.

Talon rubs his palms over his face, true betrayal and pain ringing in his eyes. "Lock is right."

Lock dips his head as if to say *naturally.*

Talon glances between Steel and Tor as if he can't bear to break this news to them. And I completely understand. Finding out your father is a monster isn't easy.

"What did it say?" Tor demands.

"Many things," Talon hurries on. "They were correspondences between Father and the Shattered Isle king." My stomach churns, but he continues. "They date back over a year." I glance at Lock, who doesn't look surprised by this at all. Talon looks at him too, visibly swallowing. "Is that why you did it?" he asks. "Is that why you left us in the night? And all your kills…"

Lock's jaw is clenched as we all turn to look at him. I lean against the glass, silently showing my support. I guessed easily enough why he did what he did, our mind sharing and bond completion practically screaming the answer at me.

"Tell them," I whisper, and his eyes meet mine. He's defiant and breaking, the pain of his brothers not trusting him shining through his eyes. He blinks, and the emotions are gone, replaced with that delicious, chaotic smile on his lips as he looks to his brothers.

"Did you really think I was slaughtering people for fun?"

The brothers look shamed by his accusation, but still utterly confused. Except for Talon, who merely looks betrayed.

"I'm lost," Tor admits.

"Father and the Shattered Isle king have been working together to seal our fates," Talon says. "Father decided our sun-blessed powers were too great a threat to his reign. With us growing closer to the age of taking over, only shy of over two hundred years, he knew he had to do something because if we challenged him for his throne, there would be no stopping us."

Steel slides down the wall, sitting with his elbows on his knees as he shakes his head.

Lightning crackles in Tor's eyes as he paces the length of the hallway.

Lock doesn't break his stoic resolve.

But Talon looks to him again. "You knew, didn't you? And the people you killed—"

"Were assassins hired to eliminate you," Lock cut him off. "Each of you," he says, looking at all of them.

"Why didn't you tell us?" Tor slams his fist on the glass, the sound vibrating through the hallway.

"I couldn't!" Lock growls, not flinching away from the lightning in Tor's eyes. "Father caught me searching his private system," he says, the breath going out of him. "I've always had my suspicions about his thirst to maintain power over all the realms. His mind… whenever I entered it…" He shakes his head. "He's not the man you remember, Talon," he says. "After our mother's death, his heart turned cold. And the years separating the events have dulled him of emotions beyond the need for power. So I went looking for solid evidence against him. I knew I needed it if I were to convince you three to join me in claiming our birthright early," he continues. "He didn't know how deep I'd dug in his system, and I covered my tracks easily enough. But he *knew* I'd seen him for the man he'd turned into, a twisted ruler fueled by greed. One that matched the king he so despised ages ago." Lock looks at me apologetically, but I wave him off. "I didn't have the proof, and I had to run. I saw it in his mind, his plot to kill me before I could tell the three of you. So, I planted a back door in his system, just like you taught me, brother, and I intercepted every encoded message from then on out. Yes, I *ran*, but I slaughtered every would-be assassin father hired to dispose of you three."

The air is heavy between the five of us as he continues. "Until one message came through about a marriage between the two realms. I thought perhaps Father had tired of his quest for blood and power, but I knew there was only one way I could find out. One way I could come home and reunite with my brothers."

"You let us catch you," Talon finishes for him.

Lock dips his head.

Steel rises, crossing to the distance to stand in front of the glass. "Open the doors," he demands, and Talon doesn't hesitate.

The glass doors *whoosh* open, and Lock releases a dark chuckle before stepping into the hallway with us. He opens his arms, that cocky grin on his face unfaltering as he says, "Surprise." He looks at each of them. "I'm not the villain."

Tor is the first to break, jerking Lock into a firm hug. Then Steel, who hugs them both, and finally Talon, who hugs them all. Tears coat my eyes at the reunion, and bitterness burns my chest for the reason behind their strain.

Two selfish, *evil* kings.

After a moment of silence, I can't help but break it. "We'll have to imprison them both or kill them."

The brothers break out of their embrace to face me.

"She's right," Lock says. "Neither will stop until we're dead. The threat we pose to their thrones is too great."

"I know," Tor says, and Talon nods.

Steel takes the longest to respond, but he finally relents. "We land at the palace in less than a day."

"We'll have to act like we don't know the king's plans," I say, then look to Lock. "And we'll have to pretend like you're still a prisoner."

"I can stand the cage for one more day, darling," he says at my look of worry.

"We take them down quietly," I say. "First, the All Plane king, then once you've secured your throne, we travel to the Isle." At least we won't have to fight them both at once. That gives us an edge.

"I don't want to spill All Plane blood if I don't have to," Steel says. "Our armies do not know of Father's discrepancies."

"Agreed," Talon and Tor say at the same time.

"When do we act?" I ask, needing a solid plan.

Talon sighs. "Father will expect us to present you first as our new princess," he says. "According to tradition, there will be a banquet held in your honor. After that, he'll expect me to bring in Lock for public shaming and execution."

I recoil at the thought, rage flowing in my veins and a protective barrier curling around the bond I have with Lock. He hisses delightfully, as if he can feel me coiling my strength around that connection between us, and he slides a hand possessively over my back. I shift into the touch, relishing the contact.

"The banquet then," I say, focusing, and they all nod.

"It'll be lax on security," Talon explains.

"Because all the armies and guards will be half drunk in celebration. Father's guard will probably be down as well because he'll believe us to be reveling too," Tor says.

"Good," I say. "We act like we're indulging in the festivities, and then—"

"You will release me," Lock cuts me off. "I will be the one to do it."

"No," Talon argues.

"I will," Lock stops him. "I'll do my best to trap him, imprison him, but you all know his strength. The fight will likely lead to..." He swallows hard. "None of you need to bear this weight. I've become accustomed to killing. One more will not ruin my already broken soul."

I place my hand on his chest. "It isn't broken," I say, and his eyes lock on mine, begging to differ.

"I'll do it," he says again. "He won't be expecting me to be free, especially if he inspects my cage beforehand himself." There is a dark determination in his eyes. "I'll slip into his mind after the banquet. He won't know what hit him."

A shudder races down my spine, but I nod. Talon, Tor, and Steel relent after some time.

"Okay," I say. "All we have to do is make it through the banquet." And after that? The Shattered Isle. I can't help that the notion terrifies me more than this, but if I know my father... he'll be... ruthless to say the least. He'll go for the hurt, not the kill, and right now, the only thing that can hurt me is an attack on my mates.

Fear rears up inside me, icy and tangible, nearly choking me. They are the things I can't lose in this world.

"We'll survive this," Steel says. "Together, we'll bring peace between all the realms."

Tor nods, and Talon follows suit.

Lock and I look at each other, two reflections of darkness. Because we both know the taste of death and betrayal and pain in a way the others do not. I interlace my fingers with his, squeezing in support. He grips me and nods to his brothers despite the wariness in his eyes. We know this won't be easy, won't be like the previous battles we've fought before, but I refuse to point that out as we stand united in the hallway.

Instead, I look each of them in the eye, silently promising them that I'll defend and support them with everything that I am.

Because they're my mates, and there is nothing more worth fighting for.

21
CARI

"We all understand our roles?" Talon asks as the ship nears the docking station at the palace of the All Plane.

"We've gone over it nonstop through the night, Tal," Tor says, folding his massive arms over his chest. "Think we've got it."

"It has to be seamless," he says, and I know he's right. One wrong move, one inkling of the king figuring out what we're up to, and he'll sic his considerable armies on us to where even we can't overpower them.

A shiver races down my spine. I won't allow that to happen.

I look at Lock, who has been uncharacteristically quiet in his cage. It kills all of us to see him back in there, but for now, we all have our roles to play.

"When will you alert Father that I'm in here?" he asks.

"After the receiving ceremony," Talon answers. "It will be my good news for him."

I clench my jaw. "I'm shocked you didn't tell him before now."

Talon narrows his gaze at me, his dark eyes promising delicious punishment for taking that tone with him. I welcome the warm desire flittering through me, let it melt the icy terror coating my insides. Talon arches a brow at me. "The information is too sensitive—"

"Bullshit," I cut him off, and his eyes flare. Tor hisses, and Steel barely covers his laugh. "You didn't tell him because you knew deep down that Lock was innocent."

"I wouldn't go that far, darling," Lock counters, and I roll my eyes.

"Admit it," I demand.

"Fine," Talon relents. "I didn't tell our father because I couldn't decide if I was going to cut him loose before we landed or not. Happy?"

I smile up at him, nodding to show him I was.

Silence settles over us, our heartbeats ticking away the time. Talon leaves first, likely to go manually pilot the ship into the palace docking station. Tor leaves second, managing with effort to hide the lightning in his eyes. Steel is the last to go, nodding at Lock, then me, before he disappears.

Heavy.

Everything feels so damn heavy.

"I wish things were different," I whisper, sliding down to sit in front of the glass wall separating Lock and myself.

He mimics my movements, and something warm unravels inside me at his willingness to sit with me on this level.

"Would you rather you stayed on the Isle?" he asks, no judgment in his tone.

"I loved living under the stars," I admit. "Loved the villages, my people. There were many things I didn't love, but the land, the midnight sea, that I will miss." I sigh, looking into his eyes. "But I would not change where I am now," I say. "I wouldn't trade any of you for all the stars in the sky. I just wish you and your brothers weren't pitted against your father. I wish mine wasn't a monster. I wish you didn't have to do what you must tonight."

If I could spare him that pain, I would. And maybe there is a way—

"I will do anything to protect my family," he says, and he's more than proven that. What he's done all this time, slaughtering assassins and letting his father spread the rumors that he killed innocents, painting Lock as a monster when he himself was the worst of all was horrific.

"I will too, Lock," I say, pressing my hand against the glass. The ship's movement stops, whirring sounds groaning far outside of it as the ship docks. Anxiousness flares in me like a flock of terrified birds, but I close my eyes and breathe deeply to calm them down. "No matter what," I say, returning my eyes to his. "Not matter what happens, I will fight for you. For Steel and Tor and Talon. For *us*."

"Darling," he says, his eyes finding the floor. "If things go south, if they go awry—"

"They won't," I vow.

"If they do," he continues anyway. "I want you to know that I've found very little happiness in this cruel world, but you..." He visibly swallows, looking at me. "You were the brightest spot in my life. A glittering star in a sea of endless dark."

Emotion clogs my throat, and I try to find the words to stop him from saying such things, from speaking like he's saying goodbye. But he knows better than me how strong the All Plane king is. It's how he's held absolute control across the realms since The Great War two hundred years ago.

"And if the worst should happen," he goes on, and it feels like he's slowly flaying me open. "I want you to leave us." My eyes widen at him. "I want you to run. I want you to beg and cheat and steal, if that's what it takes. Lie your way out of it… but you *escape*. You live. If we fall, you must save yourself—"

"Stop," I beg, tears spilling down my cheeks.

He trails his fingers along the glass as if he might catch those tears if he weren't locked up. "Promise me, darling," he demands, and I shake my head.

"I can't—"

"You *must*," he cuts me off, his tone sharp. "I can't bear to think of anything happening to you. You must promise me you'll run at the first sign of danger." I scrunch my brow at him. "I know it goes against your nature, Cari. I know how fucking strong you are. But *I* won't survive it if something happens to you. I won't be able to concentrate if I'm worried about you. Promise me?" he begs.

I see the fractures in his eyes, sense the terror along the bond. He's laying himself bare before me, opening his heart in a way he's never done with anyone before, and I can't spit on that gift.

So, I do the only thing I can to satisfy him.

I lie.

"I promise," I say through my tears, hating the bitter taste of the lie on my tongue. Because I won't ever make good on it. If things go south, I'll fight to my last breath to save them. But the plan will work. It *has* to work. We were brought together for a reason, and no amount of kings will strip us apart.

Lock sighs, his shoulders loosening a fraction. I hear more machine sounds, the ship shuddering as Talon takes it through its docking procedures. "I have to go," I whisper as I press my forehead to the glass.

Lock does the same, and I swear I can feel his heat through it. I'm desperate for more of him, his relentless passion that threatens to consume me when I'm in his presence, but I'll have to earn it first.

I feel his influence at the edge of my mind, a soothing request. I open for him mentally and gasp as he slides into my mind, his snow and stars scent gliding effortlessly to gild all of my frayed nerves. And suddenly the glass isn't between us, we aren't even on the ship anymore. We're on a smooth strip of black rock, high on a mountaintop with nothing but an endless sea of stars before us. And in the vision, I can feel nothing but love as he holds me against his chest, whispering sayings of courage and promises for the future.

"Cari, it's time," Talon's voice calls to me from the end of a long tunnel, and the surrounding vision evaporates.

"I'll see you soon," I say to Lock, thanking him with my eyes as I hurry down the hallway.

I can't bear to say goodbye.

Because I'm not naïve, I know the fight ahead of us will be a hard one. But we will win, in the end. We have a plan, and we'll execute it with perfection so the All Plane king won't know what hit him.

I draw on the confidence Lock helped instill within me, and with each step toward the main exit of the ship, I become the princess everyone expects. My gown pools at my feet and whispers against the ground as I stop before my mates. All three are waiting for me, their All Plane uniforms matching my gown in tones of gold and white. I smooth my features, meeting each of their gazes as Talon's hand hovers over the button for the main hatch.

"We ready?" he asks one last time, and when each of us nod, he presses down on the button.

The hatch unfolds itself from the ship, as it has done so many times on this journey. Opening up to a world I never knew existed and one I desperately want to continue exploring. With my mates at my side, and peace in my heart.

I take a deep breath, planting nothing but the doting, submissive wife mask on my face as the hatch lowers still.

Talon and Steel head down the long opening first, as is the planned custom, with Tor on their heels. They'll wave to the cheers of their people and then they'll announce me, allowing me only to reveal myself when the crowd is hushed.

I hold my breath as the three of them clear the hatch and step foot on their native soil. The gold ground shimmers even from this far distance, and I wait for the cheers of their people.

Silence makes my heart falter as the three of them disappear. I wait, my pulse thundering in my ears—

Screams ring out. Terrifying, *angry* screams.

"Run!" Tor yells, the rage in his voice ricocheting up the hatch.

I race to an overlooking window, and the blood freezes in my veins.

The All Plane king is there, his armies stretched behind him and blending with a group of soldiers I know all too well.

My *father's* soldiers.

And my father, standing to the right of the All Plane king. His eyes searching, no doubt, for *me*.

Four dozen armed soldiers swarm my mates, forcing them into submission with chains of unyielding iron. The surprise of the attack matched by the numbers is too much for them to overthrow.

Talon is screaming, or trying to, but it's like someone is choking him. I *know* whose invisible hand it is, and I see red. My father, wielding his dark power over my mates.

"Find my daughter!" my father yells, and a dozen guards storm the ship as the rest haul my mates into the palace.

I spin on my heels, racing through the ship, taking back hallways and stairs. Silent as a cat, so none of the guards can hear me.

I skid to a halt in front of Lock's cell. He's on his feet, concern and rage hardening his eyes.

"My father and yours," I say, cursing myself for not getting the code to his cell from Talon. "An ambush. They're searching the ship for me."

HER VILLAINS

"Fuck," he growls, and I press my hand to the control panel. "They must've known the second my brothers stepped off the ship that you failed in your assignment and went with their own plan B."

I nod, anger simmering in my veins like a poison. I thought we'd have time. Thought we'd be able to fight them separately and on our own terms.

The image of them hauling my mates away plays over and over in my head. I hear the guards' pounding footsteps on the floors above.

"Cari," Lock pleas as the footsteps get closer. "Now is the time to *run*."

I look at him for only a moment, my heart aching as the footsteps are all too close now.

"Cari," he warns.

"Forgive me," I say, and take off down the hallway, sliding between a crevice wedged in the corner of two doors leading to the mechanical rooms. I know this ship inside out, thanks to my first order of business the second I set foot aboard it.

And I assume the guards know it too, but it won't matter. They'll be distracted by the sight of their long-lost prince. I hear Lock sigh, his relief so powerful coiling down the bond. He thinks I ran. He thinks I've made good on my promise.

"Over here!" a guard yells, and the footsteps turn into running thumps as they near Lock's cage.

"Hello, boys," Lock says, his voice pure mischief and boredom. "Any of you know the code to let me out?"

The footsteps stop and I can picture all twelve of the guards settling into the hallway. "We have orders to kill on sight," a commanding voice calls out. "By the order of the All Plane king, Lock, ex-prince of the All Plane, I sentence you to death for your traitorous—"

"Yes, how sad," he cuts off the commander. "But the thing is, you need to let me out to kill me, and seeing as how none of you have moved toward the panel, I'm guessing you don't know the code."

"Think again," the commander says, and I can hear the soft beeping of a code being punched in.

Perfect. I draw ice to my hands and fashion daggers embedded with hate and rage.

The glass doors whoosh open as I silently creep behind the wall of guards. All twelve are focused on Lock, whose eyes are gleaming with the promise of death. Then they sharpen to something animalistic as three of the guards advance on him with swords drawn.

The breath leaves my lungs as they swing those swords toward him when he has no weapon to defend—

Their blades clang against a sword made entirely of shadow, and combined with his strength, he throws all three of them backward. They stumble into their fellow guards, and an all-out brawl breaks out in the hallway.

Lock sends two of the advancing guards hurtling into the walls so hard their bodies indent it.

I creep up behind the handful of guards who watch, maintaining a perimeter at the edge of the hallway so Lock can't escape.

The ice of my blades meets their necks.

One, two, three.

Each of them falls with a heavy thud as their blood spills upon the floor. The four remaining close to me spin around, drawing their swords and rushing toward me with a fury lining their faces at the sight of their fallen soldiers.

And part of me feels the sticky guilt of having their death on my hands, knowing that Steel didn't want to shed All Plane blood. But they were trying to kill Lock, my *mate*, and I will not stand for it.

Their blades meet my ice, the power in my veins unrelenting as the life of my mate is threatened. I draw more blades from my hands, frozen knives sinking into their mark with each flick of my wrist—through the eyes, the throat, or straight to the heart, the soldiers fall.

Lock is still focused on the commander before him, the strongest of the group, and the last man standing as the other bodies litter the floor.

The breath heaves in my lungs from the fight, but I step over the pile of bodies scattered along the hallway, making my way to him—

An angry roar chills my blood, halting my progress. The commander slides his blade over Lock's arm, just barely missing his *neck*.

Everything in my world narrows to the sight of Lock's blood splashing upon the floor. And when the commander grins and draws his sword back? Aiming for Lock's head?

I lose my fucking mind.

I don't breathe, don't *think*, before I'm there. Barreling in front of that raised sword, placing myself between Lock and the commander so fast neither of them has a second to react.

His sword crashes heavily against the ice of my dagger, the sheer strength of this massive male enough to bring me to my knees.

"Cari!" Lock screams behind me, his hands reaching for me.

"The little whore is protecting you. How cute," the commander says, drawing his sword back and preparing for a killing blow.

But his arrogance makes him blind to the dagger I've fashioned in my left hand, much smaller than the one in my right, but just as deadly as I sink it into the soft part of his throat. His eyes widen in shock, his sword clanging against the ground as he claws at the knife in his throat.

His knees hit the ground, and he looks up at me in shock before he falls down face first.

I stumble backward to avoid going down with him, and two firm hands haul me even farther back.

"You promised!" Lock accuses, whirling me around so hard and fast I yelp. Tears coat his eyes as we drop to our knees in an embrace. "You promised me you'd run!"

I cling to him, shaking my head as I tremble in his arms. "I couldn't," I say, breathless. "I can't lose you."

His hold on me tightens, and we both turn our heads to look at the line of bodies we left in the hallway. I move out of his hold, shifting to tear some material off my gown and make quick work of binding the wound at his arm. It's shallower than I originally thought, which brings me some relief.

"You're a devious, terrible little liar. How am I ever to trust a promise from you again?" he asks, but his eyes are all taunting chaos again.

"I guess you're just going to have to live long enough to find out," I tease right back.

Darkness settles over his eyes, and mine match his as we stand up. "More will come when you're not found so easily," he says.

"Too bad they won't find me," I say, and he smirks down at me. "Or you."

We race through the ship, my hand firmly in Lock's as he leads us through back passages and stairwells, diving deeper into the belly of the ship instead of going up. "They took your brothers," I say when we've caught our breath.

"Father won't kill them in front of all the guards," he says. "Too many are loyal to my brothers. He'll have to show proof of their treason first. Then he'll have them executed."

A low growl rumbles my chest. "Good," I say, and he cocks a brow at me. "That gives us plenty of time to stop him and my father. I'll take their heads if I have to."

"Fuck, I love you," he says, hauling me against him in the cramped space. His lips crush mine, their assault brutal in the most beautiful way. The kiss ignites a fire inside me that has me aching for more, but he draws back just as quickly.

"Together?" he asks.

"Together."

He turns, leading me through an exit shaft at the bottom of the ship, and with the cover of night on our side, we slip toward the massive golden palace on the hunt for blood.

22
TALON

*L*ightning snaps and thrashes throughout our containment cell, a bolt nearly clipping me as it reverberates off the walls.

"Will you fucking *stop* already?" I growl at Tor for what feels like the eighth time since we were thrown in here.

He roars back, but his lightning ceases. Steel already tried his strength against the cell door, but it's solid and enforced by Father's magic. There will be no breaking out from the inside.

I rake my hands over my face, hating the betraying thoughts splintering my mind. Cari's father is here, and from the way he stood next to my father, it's like he knew she would fail in her mission to kill us. Almost as if that was the plan all along—

"Stop," Steel demands. "This isn't on her."

I glare at him, wondering if I spoke some of my thoughts out loud.

"She wouldn't betray us," Tor chimes. "I fucking hope she ran like I told her to."

It's the one word he got out before the Shattered Isle king's powers overtook our voices, holding the very breath in our lungs hostage.

"Why is her father here, then?" I can't help but present the alternative solution. It's just my nature. My brain spins every angle until I'm exhausted from it.

"Because our father has been working with him behind our back for over a year," Steel says.

I can't deny that truth, but my heart is rebuilding all the walls I tore down for her. Because this feels a lot like a setup.

"He's right," Tor says. "She wouldn't do this to us."

I sigh, hoping they're right. "Either way," I say. "We have to come up with a new plan."

"When they come to get us for the execution," Steel says, and I cringe. Father is likely already appearing before the All Plane council, presenting evidence of us working against him, a string of fake accusations and evidence of our deceitful plans to go against the All Plane ways of peace and slaughter the smaller realms in a move for absolute power. "We rush them and fight our way free."

"Sounds like a good plan to me," Tor agrees, and I shake my head.

"You know he'll send more guards than we can handle on our own. We need a better strategy—"

A banging sound on the other side of the door cuts off my words. Tor and Steel flank my left and right side. The banging continues, the door rattling on its fucking hinges.

Had Father sent one of the All Plane beasts to eat us in our cell? Or is it a Shattered Isle monstrosity coming to clean its teeth with our bones?

I look at each of my brothers, a silent communication of love and support, no matter what happens. They return the gesture just as the door slams into the wall behind us, barely missing taking off our heads with it. The entryway border is covered in ice, and when the cold fog from it clears, my mouth drops.

"Let me guess," Lock says, with Cari at his side. "Talon was just forcing you two to strategize?"

Cari laughs.

"You know it," Tor says, clasping his arm with Lock's in appreciation.

Cari races into Steel's arms before tugging me and Tor into the hug. Lock merely watches, clearly having come with her himself.

"You got him out?" I ask as we break out of the embrace.

"She saved my life," he answers for her. "Even though I made her promise to run."

She gives us a predator's grin. "I'm never running from any of you," she says, then something dark and delicious flickers in her gaze. "Unless it's a game you want to play," she teases, and I swear I fucking want to drop to my knees and worship this female right now. I silently swear to never doubt her again.

"You caused quite a scene," Lock says, eying the door. "They'll have heard that."

I nod to my brothers and our wife. "Plan?"

"I'm going after my father," Cari says. "You go after yours."

"Teams?" Lock offers.

Tor and Steel nod.

"I'm going after our father," Lock says. "Talon, you with me?"

"Absolutely," I say, and after the shit he'd just pulled? I've more than come to terms with ending him.

"Tor and Steel," Cari says. "You cover the guards—"

"What?" Steel cuts her off.

"No," Tor says at the same time.

Cari sighs. "I don't need you to fight my battles for me."

"It's not about that," Steel says, taking her hand in his. "You're our mate. We're with you until the end. No matter what, and whatever we must face. Don't you get that?"

Tears color her eyes as Tor steps to her other side. Lock and I step in front of her. Together we create one unbreakable unit. "Let's finish this," I say. "On our terms."

"Together," Steel says.

The rest of us voice our agreement, even Cari.

And we turn as one to take on the world.

23
CARI

With the brothers' intimate knowledge of their palace home, it doesn't take us long to make our way unseen to the upper levels. Just as we suspect, our fathers are on this level, but unlike we were expecting, they're in the same room.

"The royal receiving room," Lock whispers in my ear as we stay hidden in the shadows just outside the grand double doors leading to the great room. "Where Father presents important matters to his council. The council have the ears and hearts of our people—nothing happens in the All Plane without their approval or endorsement, regardless of my father's wishes."

I swallow hard. There are four guards outside the door, two on either side, and there is a half dozen royal council members stationed at a round table inside the great room, all listening intently to the words of the All Plane king.

Ice crystalizes in my palms as I shift slightly and see my father in full Shattered Isle armor sitting in a chair behind the king.

"I've tried to protect my sons," the All Plane king says as he paces before the table. "For far too long, I've shielded their deceitful ways from each of you, and for that, I apologize."

Tor rolls his eyes at the same time I do. But a deep wound opens up in Steel's that I want instantly to heal, but know it will take a lot more than me to soothe this sting of betrayal.

"A father's love runs deep," he continues, motioning behind him to my father. "As I'm sure the Shattered Isle king can attest. He gave us his own daughter to bring peace between our realms, but she betrayed him just as much as my sons betrayed me. Their thirst for power has become too great, and they intended to wipe us out, take our thrones, and then rule with an iron fist over all the realms." A collective murmur rings through the council members, and the king raises a hand to silence them.

Anger boils in my stomach like acid. The king's speech is so believable because part of it is true, only they are his plans, not his sons or mine.

"Can their lives be spared?" a young female council member asks.

"No," my father says before the king can respond, and my heart lurches in my chest. My emotions war at a rapid speed. I've had the length of my journey to the All Plane to learn the monstrous history of my father, but it's hard to erase a lifetime of memories, even if many of them are tainted now. "They must be executed. And soon. Their collective powers are too great, and both our peoples are at stake."

"Have you had any leads on your son Lock?" another member asks, and the All Plane king shakes his head.

"He still poses a great threat to us," he says. "But I have all confidence in my finest soldiers' intel that they're closing in on his location near the Air Realm."

Lock cocks a brow at me, the facial expression equal parts annoyed and arrogant.

"You truly will see your sons executed?" the female member presses, and something shifts in my chest. From some of the expressions on the members' faces, not all on the council are okay with slaughtering their princes.

The All Plane king glares at her. "Would you rather I allow them to overthrow me? Allow them to take over all the realms and have millions of innocent people die in their quest for power?" He takes a steadying breath, waving his hands over some light on the round table, triggering a holographic image to spread out before them. "I intercepted these plans while my sons brought their new wife home—"

"Have your guards located her yet?" another member dares to interrupt him.

"No," he says with finality. "The princes' sky ship is a large vessel, but it's only a matter of time before she's weeded out." He points to the images before them. "Now, these plans show details of exploitation across the realms for all their valuable commodities. They intend to strip the freedoms of the realms and seize over ninety percent of their goods for themselves, leaving the realms with little to feed and provide for themselves."

"But Tor and Steel's *feed the realms* efforts have had massive positive effects over the past decade," the female member counters. "Why go to such lengths to replenish the realms' needs at their own cost if this is their end game?"

I like this female. I glance at my mates, and their eyes echo my sentiment. Not all the members sitting on this council deserve to die. Perhaps none of them do. Which means we need to wait until our fathers are alone to strike.

Though, with our breakout from the cells below, we didn't really have the luxury of waiting.

"It's a cover!" the king growls, and the female sits up straighter in her chair. She doesn't cower from his tone, which I immediately respect and admire. He jabs a finger at the fake evidence before him. No doubt those plans are replica correspondences between him and my father. "The evidence is here. I've explained things. The Shattered Ilse king has explained them. It's time to vote." He looks at each of them. "Now, do you stand with your king or against him?"

Shit. Worded like that. The council members are basically making a vote for their life or against it, not just those of me and my mates.

Four votes stand with the king, and two against. The king plants the two opposed with a punishing gaze, and the tang of fear coats the room. Lucky for those two, these two kings will never have time to carry out their grand scheme to murder us.

"It is decided," the All Plane king says. "Leave us."

Lock ushers me to the side, leading all of us farther down the hallway and into a small alcove cloaked in shadow. The footsteps of the council members sound a few moments later, and Lock holds a finger to his lips before he pushes against an intricately carved floral design on the wall of the alcove.

With a whispering hiss, a hidden door unlatches, and he gently opens it, continuing to lead us through a cramped passageway that ends in a corner of the grand room, its position concealed by elaborate red and gold drapery.

"Interesting," my father says, and I try not to so much as breathe to give away our dangerously close position to the kings. "My council doesn't dare interrupt me or challenge my decisions."

"That's because you slaughter anyone who opposes you," the All Plane king counters. "And I prefer to keep my dark deeds where they belong. *Buried.* My people love me. They adore me because they believe me to be just and wise and compassionate like in the days of old."

"And yet time has twisted your heart," my father says, and I hear him rise from his chair to cross the room. "Turned you into something closer to my likeness than those of your fathers before you."

"I'm nothing like you," the All Plane king hisses. "This is a business partnership. You overstep."

"Apologies, all great and wise king," my father taunts. "When the blood has settled, you better make good on your promises. You will not win another war against me."

Cold skates over my skin at the truth in the threat. Father has spent all this time amassing an army that will hardly be beaten.

"You will get full control of the Water and Fire realms," the king says. "I will take Earth and Air. Our territories will be equal, for once."

"My men are ready to train Water and Fire to rise to the level of the lethal Shattered Isle standards. Call for your sons. We will execute them before they can break free. Then we'll deal with my daughter."

The king calls to one of his guards, ordering him to bring his sons to him.

We're out of time.

My heart pounds so hard in my chest, I worry they can hear it across the room.

"Having second thoughts?" the All Plane king asks, and I wonder what he sees on my father's face to ask such a question.

"No," my father says. "If she were truly my daughter, she would've completed her task before landing, and we would be having a different conversation about her position in the new realms we're creating."

"I told you she would have a hard time assassinating my sons. They're formidable males."

"And yet not formidable enough to keep them alive."

"Such are the burdens of a king," the king answers, and hate coils in my stomach. How easy it is for the two of them to stand there and discuss our deaths like we're no more than cattle.

I glance to Lock, then Tor and Steel and Talon. They each wear a mixture of anguish and betrayal, pain and loss on their faces. I assume mine mirrors theirs, but I'd been raised to be a killer, so perhaps it makes it easier to picture sliding my dagger across my own father's throat for me.

A buzz of energy zaps along all four bonds inside me, and I know it's time. The guards will return any minute to tell of our escape, and we don't want to face the kings and their guards as well.

As one, we peel the drapery back, each of us fanning out to cover all exits of the room.

"Father," Lock says, and the kings whirl in our direction, eyes wide. "I've missed your cold, black heart."

The All Plane king opens his mouth to yell for the guards, but Talon is there, a blade to his throat, stopping him.

Steel and Tor stand before the doors, shutting them with a loud thud.

"Daughter," Father says, and I glare at him as I span the distance between us.

"No longer," I say, brandishing a long sword of ice and pointing it at him. "You gave up the right to call me that the second you put me on that ship."

There is no fear in his eyes, confident asshole that he is. He stares me down, more intrigued than anything. He sniffs the air between us, his nose curling up in disgust. "You completed all your bonds," he says, shaking his head. "Filthy whore. And here I thought you might actually prove useful for once."

The words hurt despite the detachment I already feel for him, but I throw up a wall of ice around my heart. "Enough," I say. "Any last words?"

"A few," he says, his tone light and casual, as if we're discussing breakfast options. "Do you think killing me is the best idea?" he asks. "I mean, I admire your efforts, but I trained my council and my armies to answer only to me. They will not bend to your will."

I bare my teeth at him. "They will when I bring back your head as a trophy. It's the Shattered Isle way, and they've known me as their sole princess for some time now."

Fear finally coats his eyes.

The All Plane king groans as he shoves Talon back with his powers.

Bands of invisible power lash around my ankles, jerking my feet out from under me so hard my head bounces off the marble floor. Stars coat my vision for a few seconds, the room spinning before I scramble upright again.

"Took you long enough," Father growls at the king, who is locked in a battle of power with Talon and Steel. Grunts and wails cry out as their powers clash, and a burst of white-hot lightning cracks through the room, barely missing the king as he dances around his sons' attacks.

Lock is at my side, urging me upward, but I shove him to the side as Father lunges for me. He's four times my size and fast. His hand closes around my throat, and he hauls me up and up until my feet dangle off the floor.

"Pathetic," he says, shaking his head as he squeezes the air from my lungs. "The next heir I sire will be twice the Shattered Isler you are."

I gape at him, feigning fear and panic in my eyes. He's forgotten that *he* trained me since I was a child, and I am more than the assassin he raised.

I'm a princess of the Shattered Isle.

A princess of the All Plane.

And I will not die here today.

I go limp in his grip, hearing the wails and roars of my mates as their king holds them captive with his power as they try to claw their way to me. Father sees the move as weakness, as me giving up, and I look into his eyes then. *Really* look. They're as cold as the ice in my veins. No remorse, no regret.

"Father," I gasp from around his tight grip, my heart rate slowing.

Nothing. Not even a twitch of emotion.

Well, that makes it easier.

I open my palms, and spears of solid ice shoot from them, sliding into his gut.

He drops me, and I land on my feet, gulping in the sweet air. Shock fills his eyes as he yanks the spears out, his blood spattering along the polished floor. He sinks to his knees, putting him at my eye level, and he swings a massive arm at me, trying to grab me again.

"Goodbye," I say, and swing an axe of pure ice across the air between us.

It stops an inch shy of his throat, his dark power holding it on an invisible wind. He glares up at me, a twisted smile on his face.

I try and yank the sword from his invisible grip, but he's too strong.

He scans the room, calculating the odds of winning this battle with the wounds I've already given him.

"You're dead," he whispers, groaning as he rises to his feet. Blood trickles from his wounds, darkening his clothes. "And if your mates survive? I'll keep you alive just long enough to have you watch me kill every single one of them." A wave of his power hits me in the chest, and I fly across the room.

My vision splinters, the room spinning from the impact as I lay limp on the floor. I see my father run through the doors, every inch of my body screaming to get up and chase after him.

Steel roars, the anguished cry snapping my attention back to the center of the room.

The All Plane king has my mates pinned, but sweat is beading from his brow at the effort it's taking him to contain them.

Life floods back to my limbs, my instincts roaring to help my mates.

"Stop!" I scream, managing to climb onto shaky legs. "You're killing them! They're your sons!"

The king whips his head to mine. "If they wanted to live as sons of mine, they should never have been so powerful. Their very existence threatens my reign, so they must die." He jerks his hand toward my mates, and their groans increase.

I see red as I storm toward the All Plane king in a fury. His great power may pin down my mates, but he didn't see me as worthy enough to fight. His mistake.

A spear of ice sinks into the hand he wields against my mates, snapping that invisible power flowing through him. He snarls at me, eying the spear that went clean through his hand, pinning it into that marble floor. He tries to jerk it free, but I send another spear, and another, until I pin his other hand and legs to the floor.

My mates sigh as they're released from the terrible power, rising to their feet and rushing toward me.

I fashion an ice axe to the king's throat, looking to my mates for their approval. This is their father, and I won't take away their choice. If they want him to live and rot in a magically concealed prison, then I will support that.

"My father," I say, panting. "He's running. I have to go after him."

Lock reaches for me, his hand sliding over mine that grips the axe. I relent, giving him the weapon as my chest heaves.

"Go with her," Lock demands of his brothers. "I'll be right behind you."

My heart clenches, but I spin on my heels, barreling for the door. Steel, Tor, and Talon are right behind me, but I spare a look over my shoulder once we reach the door. Just in time to see Lock haul the axe up and bring it slicing down in one graceful strike.

And the All Plane king's head hits the floor.

24
CARI

My feet pound against the marble floor as I race through the palace, heading for the sky ship dock we came in on as fast as I can run.

"Left!" Steel hollers right before he passes me with his speed, leading us the quickest way through the palace.

A loud rumble sounds from just outside the palace, a sound I recognize as my father's sky ship.

"He's getting away!" I yell.

"No, he's not!" Tor hollers defiantly, lightning lighting up the hallway as we follow Steel through two massive doors.

I skid on golden sand, dropping to my knees as I watch my father's sky ship launch into the night sky. "No!"

Tor fires bolt after bolt of lightning, but the speed of the ship is too fast, and it soon disappears. My father escaped, taking the small army he brought with him back to our home.

"Fuck," I snap, slamming my fist against the ground as I rise to my feet.

"We'll follow him," Talon says, his voice calm to my chaos.

I suck in a sharp breath, nodding. "*Lock*," I say, turning back to the palace.

We left him alone. After what he'd done, we left him. And he hadn't followed us like he said he would. My breath catches as worry shoots through me. We hurry back through the halls, back to the grand room—

Guards fill the space, weapons pointed at Lock, who has his hands raised.

"Hit a little snag, darling," Lock says by way of explanation.

I break through the guards, as does Talon, Steel, and Tor, and we turn to face them as one, meeting each of their eyes with a look of unbreakable determination.

Silence fills the room except for our breathing, and I draw more ice to my palms, exhaustion settling in my bones. If I have to, I'll kill every guard who tries to hurt my mates.

"He's innocent of the crimes my father accused him of," Talon says, and as the eldest of the brothers, the guards straighten up and listen. "Lower your weapons. Now."

"And *kneel*," Lock says, smirking. "To your new kings and queen."

Weapons clatter to the floor as the guards take in the scene, and soon every single one of them is kneeling.

The council members file into the room, shock and horror on their faces.

HER VILLAINS

"We need to talk," Talon says to them, and Steel and Tor follow him toward the members.

"And I need a moment with our queen," Lock says, wrapping his fingers around my wrist and hauling me toward the passage in which we came.

The farther we make it away from the room, the more my body aches from the fight. But my soul is far worse off. I can feel the conflicting emotions mirrored across our mating bonds as well. This won't be a wound easily healed for them, but for now, I'm willing to go wherever Lock beckons.

He locks the door behind us as he leads me into a grand room painted in dark blue and black tones, and I immediately recognize his scent all over it.

"My old quarters," he says. "I felt your need for space, and I have no taste for politics."

"Thank you," I say. "Will Talon and Steel and Tor explain everything to the council then?"

"Yes," Lock says, leading me to the bathing chamber. He runs my bloody hands beneath the warm water in his sink, washing his own as well until we're both cleansed of the darkness.

"My father got away," I say.

He dries my hands. "But not before you sank your claws into him," Lock says, and a broken smile shapes my lips. "We will finish what we started," he says, leading me back into his room. "Your father will pay for his crimes, and your people will finally be freed. But first, we have to assure our position here is solidified before we abandon the throne."

"I understand," I say. My mind whirls, exhaustion and urgency settling deep inside me. I sink onto his massive bed. Tears hit the backs of my eyes, but I don't let them fall, knowing if I do, I won't be able to stop.

My father almost killed me, and I almost killed him. And now... now he'll be waiting for me to strike back—

Lock cups my cheeks in his hands, drawing me to the present. His eyes drink in mine like he's trying to siphon my pain. I lean into his touch, and he brushes his lips across mine. The kiss is a match to gasoline, igniting an internal blaze of need along our bond.

He groans against my lips as I deepen the kiss, yanking him to me in desperation.

This.

I need this.

Him.

I almost lost him twice today. Almost lost his brothers too.

My mates.

But they're whole, and he's here with me now.

I jerk back, a smile shaping my lips. "I get to keep you forever," I say, and I cling to that bright spot among all the dark.

"An eternity won't be enough with you," he says, reclaiming my mouth in a kiss.

Each caress of his hands along my body erases some of the darkness writhing in my soul.

Each kiss is a promise that we'll survive the battles ahead of us.

My heart swells as desire builds and builds inside me until I'm certain I'll die if he doesn't claim me.

"Where shall I fuck you now, darling?" he asks between kisses. "That mountain top? The ocean?"

I shake my head, tearing at his clothes like a starved female. "Here," I say, motioning to his bed. "I just want to be with you."

His eyes gutter, emotion rippling from them, with my choice to stay in this reality with him.

"Here," he echoes my sentiment, stripping me bare and splaying me on his bed like his own personal feast. He plants kisses down my chest, over my breasts, and lower until he's reached the apex of my thighs. "And here," he says, swiping his tongue over my swollen flesh.

I gasp, tangling my fingers in his hair as he devours me, pushing me over edge after edge until I can't see beyond wanting him. Needing him.

And when he finally thrusts his cock inside me, I burst into a million tiny pieces of starlight. The joining of our two souls blotting out all the dark and leaving nothing but brilliance in its wake.

My love.

My mate.

Mine.

* * *

It's hours before Lock and I are done ravaging each other, but somehow, we manage to dress in clean clothes and make our way through the palace.

I wear a gown of glistening black to match his suit, his signature hunter-green coat draped over the finery and flowing around his ankles as we walk. My long dark hair is up in a mess of braids and bun, leaving my neck and the wounds my father placed there on display.

Lock guides me to the throne room, which is packed with royal council members, staff, and guards. I keep my eyes trained forward, not sure where their loyalties lie as we make our way to where Talon, Steel, and Tor wait for us upon a raised dais at the head of the room.

There is only one throne, a massive chair carved of gold and bedecked with rubies. I eye each of them curiously as they stand around the chair instead of one of them electing to sit in it—likely Talon since he is the eldest—but perhaps they don't want to sit where their father once reigned.

Lock grips my hand, twirling me to face the crowd of onlookers as we reach his brothers, and he plops me right on the throne. I gasp from the power move, motioning to get up as I look to Talon. He shakes his head at me, smiling as he moves to stand before me. Steel hands him a crown of gold and rubies that matches the throne, and Talon positions it gently on my head.

Tears bite my eyes, and I swallow hard as I feel the love from all the bonds radiating inside me.

Talon winks down at me, then shifts to stand on my right next to Steel. Lock and Tor stand on my left.

"Bow," Lock says, his voice ringing out across the grand room. "Before your new queen."

The air freezes in my lungs as every person in the room kneels before the dais.

"Welcome home," Steel whispers in my ear. "My queen."

A warm shiver races down my spine, and Tor runs his fingers over my bare shoulder, the touch loving and supportive.

Steel does the same to my other shoulder, and Lock and Talon kneel to smooth their hands over my thighs.

A storm of love and power and hope fills me so much I want to cry out, but I reach for them and raise my chin at the onlookers.

"Together," I say loud enough for everyone to hear. "We will bring peace to the realms. Starting with the elimination of the Shattered Isle king."

A collective gasp rings out before applause replaces it, and I breathe out a tight breath as I look at my mates.

"We'll make travel and battle plans soon," Talon assures me as he waves a hand in dismissal to the people filling the room. They file out, and I breathe deeply in relief. It will take time getting used to being a... fuck, a queen. But as long as I'm *their* queen, I think I can handle it. "It will likely be a few days before we're prepared to move on the Shattered Isle," he continues, and I nod.

A few days. I can handle that. And when we get there? I'll finish what my father started, repay him every harm he would've done to me if he'd had the chance.

"Until then," Tor says, drawing me back to the resent. "Lock has monopolized enough of your time. Steel and I need to see you."

Warmth floods my core at the promise in their eyes.

Talon squeezes my thigh. "Enjoy those two today," he says. "But you'll be spending tonight in *my* bed."

Lock growls. "Then I get all day tomorrow," he says, and I laugh, because I just can't help it.

"Don't worry, mates," I say. "There is plenty of me to go around."

Their touches turn carnal, claiming, and downright primal, and I gasp as I realize this is my future unfolding before me.

Not one filled with the villains I had once pictured.

But one filled with love and passion and peace.

A peace I'll buy with my father's blood in three days' time.

Until then? I'm going to enjoy my mates.

THE END

Thank you so much for reading! If you enjoyed this and want to find out what happens next with Cari and the brothers, please be sure to pre-order HER REVENGE here and check out the sneak peek of chapter one below!

HER REVENGE SNEAK PEEK

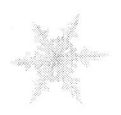

Chapter One
Cari

"You can't honestly think we need to dispatch an entire unit," Chador, one of the males on the All Plane high council, says.

He's a handful of years older than me and wears the sun emblem of All Plane royalty on his maroon shirt. He waves his arm over the circular table the council and my four husbands gather around, a holographic map of the Shattered Isle poised over the flat surface.

"The Shattered Isle king made plans with our father to execute us and take control of fifty percent of the realms," Steel says, his muscled arms crossed over his chest.

I can feel the frustration flickering down our bond from where I sit in a cushioned chair a few feet away.

"Would you have us allow that behavior to go unchecked?" Steel continues. A muscle in his jaw ticks as he stares Chador down, and a lick of heat shoots across my skin. I would never want to be on the receiving end of Steel's anger—he's calm and kind and collected so much of the time, but when he's crossed? All bets are off.

"Of course not," Chador says, rolling his eyes. "I'm merely saying you don't need to steal twenty percent of our armed forces in order to check him."

"*Steal* them?" Tor snaps, lightning crackling in his eyes. The hair on the back of my neck stands on end from the electricity rippling off of him. "We're the kings of the All Plane," he continues, his voice rough. "Not to mention I've been their head commander for longer than you've sat on this council." Chador's eye twitches at that. "If I want to send our entire army to the Air Realm for no other reason than to host a six-week course on the proper way to sharpen a blade, then that's my right."

"Six whole weeks on blade sharpening?" Lock says, arching a dark brow at Tor. "Sounds horribly dull."

"Maybe you should go alone, Prince Lock," Chador says. "You're used to killing things. This should be an easy mission for you—"

"*King*," Lock says, his eyes sharp as he glares at Chador. He turns slightly, his long hunter-green coat shifting with the movement.

I hold my breath.

Hell, even Tor holds his breath as we watch.

"As a member of the esteemed high council of the All Plane, you should be able to remember titles. If you can't, perhaps your seat would be better served with someone else sitting on it."

Chador swallows hard, then shakes his head. "Our forces need to stay here more than ever," he says and throws a desperate look at the other five council members crowded around the table. He gets two begrudging nods and three outright looks of disapproval. "With the execution of our king—"

"Our father took up arms against us," Talon says, his voice ice-cold. "We had no choice. If you have doubts, I'll replay the footage my sleeper drones captured."

Chills burst over my skin, my blood crystalizing with frost. Talon's sleeper drones—tiny, almost imperceptible robots— were stationed all over the palace. They recorded everything, an order set forth by his father centuries ago. We'd seen the footage, and had to play it several times in order to prevent a rebellion from those who thought my husbands had murdered their father for the throne. The footage proved otherwise, but watching it…

Seeing their father wield his powers against his own sons, watching him admit to ordering hits on them…

Watching my own father escape my grasp…

Ice chills my hands, adrenaline coursing through my blood, demanding action.

Chador blows out a breath, bracing his knuckles on the table. "There is no debating the footage," he says through his teeth, pointing one finger at the holographic rendering of the Shattered Isle palace.

My *home*. Its magnificent structure sits on the centermost section of our great island. The midnight ocean I love so much stretches around it for miles and miles. Something sharp pricks my chest. A sense of longing that's immediately followed by a heavy dose of shame.

"But the All Plane has never taken war lightly," Chador continues. "You show up there with enough armed forces to take the island and you'll terrify the other realms into thinking they're next. They'll start prepping for war too. It'll be chaos."

Talon glances at Steel and they hold some silent, contemplative conversation.

"You don't need the All Plane army," Chador says. "You need two good warriors. Everyone knows the Shattered Islers are soft of mind and weak of spirit, thanks to the stars and moon they worship." His nose turns up. "Take out the king once and for all, and then make plans to educate the people of the isle on the correct way—"

His words are cut off by the sound of my ice dagger sinking into the table an inch from where his hand rests.

Everyone turns their attention to me.

Lock smirks, his eyes glistening with mischief. "That was naughty, darling," he says, pride sizzling down our bond.

Chador's gulp is audible as I rise from my seat, strolling to the table. Talon and Lock immediately shift to make a place for me to stand. I focus on Chador. "It's that kind of talk that separated our two great realms for centuries," I say, tilting my head. "When was the last time you visited the Shattered Isle, Councilor Chador?"

He parts his lips, glancing at the other council members before returning his eyes to me.

"I'll take that as *never*," I say, and he presses his lips into a firm line. I nod. "Do us a favor and don't speak on subjects you know nothing about. *My* people are innocent of the crimes of my father." Most of them. Some—like Father's warriors and generals and devout followers—would face consequences, but that would be *after* we defeated my father. "And they are in no way 'soft in mind and weak in spirit.'" I roll my eyes. He didn't have a clue how amazing my people truly were. None of them did, honestly. And that's why we were here planning and strategizing to correct that wrong.

Tor grins at Chador, but there is nothing friendly about it.

"*Apologize*," Lock says, shifting so he towers over Chador.

Chador grinds his teeth, glaring at the other council members, who remain silent. "Forgive me," he says.

Lock tilts his head, an eyebrow raised. "My queen," he says, drawing out the words like he's teaching a youngling to talk.

Chador looks like he'd rather be beheaded than address me by my new title. And while the idea is tempting, it's not what he deserves.

"It's fine, Lock," I say, drawing my husband's attention. The eyes of the council members follow. "It's been one day," I continue. "It will take time for your people *and* your advisors to adjust to our new situation."

Lock purses his lips, planting me with a look that sends heat spiraling right down the center of me. "Our new situation?" He strolls up to me, sliding one finger down the side of my neck. "The one where you're our mate, our wife, our queen? *That* situation?"

I try to keep the political mask in place, but it slips, just a fraction, as I bite back a smile.

"Yes," I say, slightly breathless from the way he's looking down at me, from how close he stands.

"I can only speak for myself," Maia, the lone female council member, says. "But change has been a long time coming." She dips her head to me, then my husbands. "I stand with you because I believe you will be the change the All Plane *and* the Shattered Isle needs."

I offer her a small smile and nod. In the future, when we are granted time not hindered by battles and threats, I want to get to know her better. She showed her character by challenging the All Plane king when he tried to convince them to pass a vote to execute his sons—my husbands—and for that alone, I'll be in her debt.

"Thank you, Maia," Talon says, then glances at the other members. "I am not my father. My brothers are not my father. You have a choice now, but *only* now. If you plan to fight or oppose us because of our new alliance, then speak now or simply leave. We will not take action against you." He eyes Chador, but the male doesn't budge an inch. "If you stay, then do so knowing that Cari is our wife and your queen and you will treat her as such. From this moment on, you are loyal to her and to us."

I hold my breath, my nerves tangling. Asking them to accept me isn't a new concept—they've been prepped since the weeks before our bonding ceremony—but declaring war for their new queen is another matter entirely.

The room is silent, not even a peep from Chador, who obviously isn't my biggest fan.

"Good," Talon says, waving an arm toward the grand double doors on the opposite side of the room. "You're dismissed. We'll inform you of our final plans tomorrow."

The council members slowly file out of the room, and I breathe a little easier once the doors shut behind them.

Steel reaches over the table, yanking out my dagger embedded into the wood. He spins it in his hand, then expertly throws it across the room, the tip sinking into a beam. He turns to me, an amused look on his face.

"I know," I say before he can get a word out. "I'll do better."

Steel furrows his brow. "What do you mean?"

I sigh. "I shouldn't have reacted that way," I say, eying the new hole in the table. "It will take your people time to adjust to me. And twice as long for the lies about *my* people to fade from their minds. I can't throw a fit every time someone insults them."

"Sure you can," Lock says.

"I like it when you throw daggers," Tor adds.

I bite back a smile, but it fades when I see the serious look on Talon's face.

"I *will* do better," I vow to him.

He blinks a few times, then shakes his head. "We all have to," he says, eying the map still on the table. He rubs his palms over his face. "I wasn't expecting to go to war so soon after taking the throne." He looks at me, a broken smile on his lips. "Some honeymoon."

"We're not going to war," I say, and each of my husbands turn a curious glance my way. I swallow hard and point to the spot on the map where my dagger hit. "Those coves conceal secret entryways into the palace," I explain. "We don't need an army. If we take out my father, then most of the Shatter Isle warriors will follow me, *us*."

"Does your father know about these tunnels?" Lock asks.

"He knows about these," I say, dragging my finger through the map and around the palace, down the beach, and pause on another set of coves. I glance up at Talon, who flinches at the sight.

The same place where The Great War started, where a young Talon saw my father murder his mother. I flash him an apologetic look and return focus to the spot I'd mentioned before.

"These tunnels," I say, tapping on the spot. "I made myself."

"How?" Tor asks.

"Ice and patience and a friend sworn to secrecy," I say, a ghost of a smile on my lips.

Gessi. My friend, my handmaiden blessed with the gift of earth manipulation. We worked for months creating the tunnels that aided in our adventures outside the palace. It was our escape route for when royal pressures mounted.

"All I have to do is make it to that cove, slip inside the palace, and slit his throat." A lump forms in my throat. "No war. No warriors' lives at risk. Just me."

"You're not going alone," Steel says.

"Of course, she's not going alone," Tor agrees.

"I was raised as an assassin," I counter. "I'll be fine—"

"You never have to do anything alone ever again," Lock says.

"You're needed here," I argue. "Your people need you more than ever right now. If their kings leave, it'll be like asking for open rebellion."

"She's not wrong," Talon says, then shakes his head. "But you're not going alone. We're coming with you," he says. "You have no idea what you might face. Once your father reaches the isle, he'll surround himself with all manner of protection—guards, warriors, contraptions fueled by his powers. He knows you'll come for his head and he won't make it easy."

I don't argue, because he's right. It will be a hard fight, one I'm not sure I'll survive, but I can't let him take out his anger on our people. Which he will. He didn't expect to lose his newly formed alliance with the All Plane king so quickly—and all the realms promised to him along with it. He'll be livid, and I know right where he'll place that wrath.

My home. My people. They are innocent and I won't allow them to pay for his mistakes.

"If you four go with me," I say. "Who ensures that someone like Chador won't try to usurp the throne?"

Talon glances to Tor, and they both grin at the same time.

Steel looks between the two brothers, then nods.

"Storm," Talon says.

"And River," Tor adds.

I glance at Lock, who merely nods before leaning down to whisper in my ear. "Talon and Tor's best friends and most trusted right hands."

"They'd die before letting anyone steal the throne from us," Talon says.

"And they'll keep the peace while we're away," Tor adds.

I raise my brows at Steel. "What about your best friend?" I ask.

Steel parts his lips—

"Blaize is a liability," Talon says before Steel can speak.

"You've never given him a chance," Steel argues.

"He betrayed our father—"

"Who just tried to kill us," Steel says, his hands fisting at his sides as he faces his brother.

Talon opens and shuts his mouth a few times. "Blaize is reckless. You know that. He's a wildcard, his values shift as easily as the wind."

Steel shakes his head. "He's a good male," he says. "He's never let me down before."

"And when we return, you can appoint him your personal guard for all I care, but I will not leave the fate of our realm in his hands." Talon's words are final, and he turns to Tor. "Let's hunt down Storm and River," he says. "I'm sure father sent them and their warriors off on a mission before we returned to ensure they weren't here to defend us." He sighs, then glances at me. "We'll see you for dinner?"

I nod, my heart twisting at the tension between him and Steel.

Tor winks at me before following Talon out of the room.

I reach for Steel, but he's already moving across the room. "I need air," he grumbles, then disappears through the doors, the sound of them slamming behind him echoing through the room.

Lock whistles. "That never gets old," he says, a playful smile on his lips.

"They do that a lot?"

Lock nods. "One of the few things Talon and Steel ever fight about is Blaize." He shakes his head. "Steel rarely has blind spots, but Blaize is one of them."

"Is he truly a rogue like Talon says?"

Lock shrugs. "As much as I am, I suppose." His grin turns animalistic as he shifts closer, his hands grazing down to my hips.

I arch into his touch, gasping slightly as he draws me against his body. "We'll have plenty of time to talk about them later," he says. "Right now, there are more important things to discuss."

Flames slide over my skin as he moves me closer to the council table, lifting me so I sit on the edge. "Such as?" I ask, my heart beating wildly in my chest.

I know we *should* be preparing for our journey and for the battle we're about to face, but if I can steal a few blissful moments with him, I will.

He spreads my thighs, the silk of my dress climbing up my legs with the motion, and he steps between them. "Such as," he says, tangling one hand in my hair, the other disappearing beneath the hem of my dress. "How hard you want me to fuck you on this table."

A warm shiver dances over my body and everything inside me narrows to the feel of his fingers teasing the lace covering my heat. The featherlight touches awaken every nerve ending in my body, and I smile up at him.

"Do your worst," I challenge, and his blue-green eyes churn.

He leans down, so close our lips almost touch, and he holds me there in delightful anticipation. Tendrils of shadow curl from his shoulders, snaking down his arms until they lovingly coil around my wrists—

I'm tugged backward, my spine kissing the council table as his shadows secure my arms over my head, two more soft-as-silk wisps twining around my ankles and spreading my legs apart.

My breath is ragged as I look at Lock.

Slowly, he peels off his jacket and tosses it on the other side of the table.

Meticulously, he rolls up the sleeves of his sleek black shirt.

"You really shouldn't have said that," he says, his grin predatory as he raises his hands, shadows dripping from his fingers and curling their way over my body, teasing and torturing me with silky caresses. "Let's begin."

To Be Continued!
If you're enjoying this journey and want to read more, please pre-order HER REVENGE here!

LET'S CHAT!

I love hearing from you! You can find me at the following places!

Facebook

Facebook Author Page

Jadempresley@gmail.com

And be sure to sign up for my newsletter here for release information, cover reveals, and giveaways!

ACKNOWLEDGMENTS

A huge thank you to Amber Hodge for editing this and making it sparkle! I couldn't do this series without you! Thanks to my husband and family who always indulge me when I get lost in the writing cave. Thank you to all the amazing readers for picking this up and taking a chance on four delightfully different brothers! And finally, a huge shout out to all the Marvel fans who just want a little more sometimes :)

ABOUT THE AUTHOR

Jade Presley is a pen name for a fantasy and contemporary romance author who loves cranking out stories about seriously sexy males and the sassy women who bring them to their knees. She's a wife, mother, and board game connoisseur.

Printed in Great Britain
by Amazon